When Legends Spark

Firestarter and Swordsman
Book 1
Casey Blair

When Legends Spark
Firestarter and Swordsman Book 1

Copyright © 2024 Casey Blair,
All rights reserved.

No part of this edition may be reproduced, distributed, transmitted, or used in any manner whatsoever without permission in writing from the author, except in the case of brief quotations in a book review. For permission requests, email casey@caseyblair.com.

No AI Training: Without in any way limiting the author's exclusive rights under copyright, any use of this publication to "train" generative artificial intelligence (AI) technologies is expressly prohibited.

This book is a work of fiction. Names, characters, places, and events are either the product of the author's imagination or are used fictitiously. Any resemblance to actual persons, living or dead, events, or locales is entirely coincidental.

Developmental editing by Zola Hartley, 2024.
Proofreading by Adie Hart, 2024.
Cover design by GetCovers, 2024.
Author photo by Mariah Bush, 2013.

www.caseyblair.com

Chapter 1

The white expanse of the Frozen Wilds stretched until his eyes blurred. Kazuron kept his eyes on the emptiness as he steered the magic-powered snowglider home, even deeper into the wintry abyss.

Not empty. Soothing. He'd *chosen* to retire where no one could easily find him, after all.

So he was definitely not bored to tears.

And if he was lonely, well, that was the price he paid for being the most renowned swordsman in the Five Protectates, the collections of nations that surrounded the Frozen Wilds.

Winter was his goddamn *reprieve*, he reminded himself. The feeling would pass—or intensify—just as soon as he took another student and reminded himself how much he hated living with another person.

He did love the freedom of the Frozen Wilds, and he especially loved not having to make himself smaller—or, occasionally, bigger—for the sake of other people. He dreaded every time he had to interact with people in town. That's why he stocked up supplies for weeks at a time, so he wouldn't have to make the hours-long journey too frequently. It would be a relief to get back home where no one looked at him with fear or expectation.

Because no one was there to look at him at all.

Goddamn it.

Kazuron leaned his hand harder against the snowglider's controls, increasing the flame that burned through its magical fuel, making it speed even faster over the rolling hills of snow.

Once he was home, he could at least do *something* to distract himself from this melancholy, even if he was beginning to feel like a sword so meticulously sharpened its substance wore away.

But he definitely wasn't in the mood to get caught in a fucking blizzard, and one of the ferocious storms the Frozen Wilds was known for was fast approaching.

He remembered when even that had been novel—when no one was counting on him, and he could afford to take stupid risks. He'd loved driving no matter the weather and the feeling of contentment from the snowfall the vast majority of the year.

Now, Kazuron gazed out across the white all around him, as though if he glared hard enough the Frozen Wilds would manifest that former feeling of peace for him.

Which is the reason he saw, to his surprise, a dark spot in the snow.

Further squinting revealed people. They had a snowglider too—a bigger one than his, which meant they had funds, since even his wasn't cheap—but they weren't moving.

Kazuron frowned, shifting the angle of his own direction to bring him by them. He'd never seen vacationers this deep in the Frozen Wilds, but if they'd lost their way, run out of fuel, or not known the signs of an incoming blizzard, he could help get them on their way.

And out of his space.

Because he didn't want people interrupting his retirement.

Kazuron wasn't sure if he was grateful for the distraction or annoyed that he was going to have to make polite conversation for a second time that day or, worse, mad that he couldn't even tell, so he was scowling pretty fiercely as he closed in on them.

A scowl that, with an effort of will, he blanked from his face as they tensed when he pulled alongside what was apparently a temporary camp.

He'd been living on his own too long. He'd lost the habit of how to not intimidate people just by existing.

But Kazuron also didn't miss that they carefully moved to block his view of someone seated on the ground.

Maybe this was going to be a day for making himself bigger, not smaller.

"Afternoon, neighbors," Kazuron said.

One of the men snapped, "Can we help you?"

Bundled up as he was, Kazuron couldn't make out much in the way of his features, but the man still paced around like he was cold and on edge. It was hard to tell through all the winter clothing, but he had a sinewy build that almost looked like a desert silik from Aksola. But a silik would have to be desperate to venture into snow like this.

Silik or not, angry and defensive was not the type Kazuron would have expected to be casually eating while taking in the landscape in this weather.

On cue, the snow began to fall.

Kazuron said, "Thought you might be in need of assistance, since you're stopped here with a blizzard on the horizon."

The head of the person on the ground peeked around a leg.

Kazuron was so taken aback by the fact that she was in a short-sleeve tunic—barefoot in freezing temperatures—that it took him a second to notice she was *gagged*.

The person blocking his view of her shifted, but not soon enough.

"What in the goddamned hells," Kazuron growled, "do you think you're playing at?"

The first man stepped in front of him, blocking his vision.

Orange eyes: he *was* a silik. What in the hells?

Kazuron didn't back up. "I asked you a question."

"This doesn't concern you," the man insisted fiercely.

"I'd be delighted to believe that."

Which he should have meant. He'd retired to get out of being entangled in whatever the plot-of-the-day was with whoever had hired him, everyone always trying to play him.

But instead of feeling weary, for the first time in a long time his hand was practically twitching toward his sword.

No.

Not yet.

"Persuade me," Kazuron said in a voice like death.

Another man—definitely human this time—stepped forward, and this one wasn't on edge. The damn fool was *swaggering*.

"You want gold to stay out of this?" The new jackass snorted. "You're outnumbered, old man. We don't answer to any meathead in the middle of nowhere, and I don't see a uniform on you."

Kazuron's burgeoning anger was like a coal in his chest. If they assumed he wanted money, they were mercenaries at best,

Mercenaries were usually smarter, though. Like the first man, who was backing away from whatever he could read coming from Kazuron.

So: maybe mercenaries, but also someone both wealthy and entitled, *sheltered* enough to not recognize the death he was calling toward himself.

Whoever had paid siliks to operate here, in the height of winter, in the territory Kazuron was known to reside in, must have deep pockets. And while Kazuron had left politics behind on purpose, he didn't like that this had very nearly happened here without him knowing about it.

So much for his reprieve. He had some goddamned work to do, it looked like, because he had no idea what in the hells was going on here.

"No uniform on you either," Kazuron said evenly. "And it doesn't matter how many of you there are if I don't like your answers. You have ten seconds."

The man tried to stare him down, his eyes searching Kazuron's expression within his haughty glare.

But as the seconds ticked away, evidently some extremely buried survival instinct peeked through and he didn't like whatever he found in Kazuron's gaze, because the man finally said, "Look, this woman is an international criminal. This is a covert mission—"

The man's head slid to the ground when Kazuron drew his greatsword and sliced it off his neck midsentence.

He'd heard more than enough to understand.

And he was retired, not dead.

"So you're slavers," Kazuron said, casting his gaze around in the shocked stillness that followed, his sword ready. "Not for long."

That got them moving.

But not before Kazuron had taken down two more, faster than they could even grab for weapons—or reach for him with siliks' poison-tipped claws.

A man bellowed from behind him, and Kazuron turned to counter him only to see him literally go up in flames. Kazuron cut him down before he could stumble and spread the fire to him on his way down.

As the slaver fell, behind him the woman on the ground rose to her feet, her gag and bindings flickering away into ash without burning her as he watched.

Fuck. A fully trained firestarter to auction explained the slavers' monetary incentive, at least, if not who was funding it.

Then her fierce gaze caught his, and for a moment time stopped for him.

Sharp hazel eyes and reddish brown hair that stood out against a light dusting of freckles. Her features were pretty, but it was the expression on her face that arrested him.

This was a warrior. Full of righteous fury, and sizing him up.

His blood soared with awareness, a meeting of a kindred spirit in the heat of battle.

This kind of interaction, he knew how to handle.

Kazuron nodded at her in thanks, breaking the spell.

Time sped up again.

Another person tried to bundle the firestarter into their snowglider, and she turned and set them on fire, too, while Kazuron whirled, taking out two more attackers quickly and pressing forward. Fighting in snow this deep was a challenge even for him, and he trained here every day.

For the slavers, it was impossible.

But two of them did manage to get back to their snowglider before he could catch them, slowing him down with a crossfire bolt. He dodged, but that gave them time to fire their snowglider up and hightail it out of there.

Kazuron lowered his sword, watching them go.

But the firestarter tore past him, snow melting around her to speed her way, chasing the snowglider on foot.

A few strides in her wake took him to her side, and he caught her by the shoulder.

She tore out of his grip and glared at him.

"You'll never catch them like this," he told her.

"I was trying," she growled at him, "to see what direction they were going. So I can hunt them down later, before they hunt me."

As one, they looked back in the direction the snowglider had gone, passing out of sight under the crest of the hills all throughout the Frozen Wilds.

In the minutes the fight had taken, the snow had picked up and was coming down hard. Even taking his snowglider, by the time they followed, the slavers' tracks would be covered.

"I apologize," Kazuron said, "but there are multiple routes they could have taken from here. Is that why you were still with them? They clearly didn't know what you could do."

"Oh, they knew," she said. "I was drugged when they took me. I didn't do anything sooner because then I'd have been alone in the depths of the Frozen Wilds with no shelter and no idea where to go."

Until he'd arrived, and obviously not been their companion nor willing to step aside. Another option.

But she was glaring at him now, and he understood.

Now she was going to be forced to trust him, and while he wasn't a slaver, all she knew of him was that he was ready and able to kill at a moment's notice.

Kazuron sighed internally. Years retired, and he was still only capable of making one kind of impression.

He wiped the blood off his sword and sheathed it in one move. "My name's Kazuron. You?"

She eyed him. "Jesra."

He nodded, keeping things professional. He'd avoid making her more uncomfortable if he could.

Then again. Would keeping the sword out longer have been more threatening, or was sheathing it in a move that took so much practice worse?

He sighed, and this time it was out loud.

"There's a blizzard coming, so you'd better come with me. Once it passes, I'll take you wherever you want to go."

Jesra nodded tightly, and they trudged over to his snowglider.

Which didn't start on the first try.

Kazuron grunted. "It's all the moisture from the fresh snow, just give it a second."

"No need." Before he could press the controls again, the snowglider fired to life.

Jesra raised her eyebrows at him.

Of course. Firestarter.

Kazuron snorted. "Thank you."

"My pleasure."

As he got them going in the right direction again, Kazuron said, "If you can affect the snowglider that easily, I'm surprised they didn't keep you drugged."

"They were supposed to," Jesra said, "but the pack with the drug soaked through. They'd stopped to build a fire to dry it out, which took long enough for the previous dose to wear off completely."

Kazuron whistled. "Lucky timing."

Or deniable sabotage. Siliks were *very* sensitive to cold and wet—any one of them should have known how to keep a package dry.

"Very," Jesra agreed tonelessly. "I should have stolen your snowglider first. Then I could have chased them."

Kazuron glanced at her. She didn't know him, but he also didn't know her. She'd been kidnapped, but one of the first things he'd seen her do was burn a man to death. "Yes," he said evenly, "you could have."

Jesra sighed, and her voice when she spoke next was exhausted. "But then you'd have been stranded instead."

"Yes," he agreed, mentally standing down. "Will you make it a little while longer without warm layers?" He wasn't sure *he'd* make it without his own, but he'd figure it out if he had to.

"Yes."

Monosyllable response.

He glanced over to see her eyes had taken on a glassy look he recognized too well. Capable she might be, but this firestarter had been through an ordeal—betrayed, certainly, by someone with substantial resources; drugged, kidnapped, nearly frozen. Conversation could wait until she was ready.

Ready didn't materialize again before they arrived back at his cottage, the snowstorm picking up.

Jesra's clothes were totally soaked through, but she hadn't uttered a word of complaint, just shrunk in on herself. That worried him.

Not just how badly off she was right now, but that she'd be harder to help if she hid it from him.

Kazuron got the door to his cottage unlocked and it slammed all the way open with the force of the wind. Jesra didn't hesitate to follow him in, though she did freeze once he'd shut the door behind him.

Kazuron pretended he hadn't noticed.

"This way," he said, behaving as if there was no reason for her to not follow him. "I have a guest room for when I take students, but you'll be shocked to learn no one ever wants to come out this time of year. So that's all yours, but I only have one bathroom, through here. You should shower to warm up."

Kazuron paused at a closet in the hallway. "Clean towels."

He pressed them into her hands, then pointed. "Guest room, bathroom, my room. Dirty laundry goes in this basket here. Closet's in my room—I don't have spare clothing for guests, but take whatever of mine will fit. I'll leave you to it while I get the supplies inside and some hot food going. Come out when you're ready. All set?"

Jesra nodded once, jerkily.

Probably didn't retain all that. Kazuron nodded and left anyway, because she'd do better if she believed he wasn't watching her. If she needed to break down, or time to nerve herself up to stripping in a stranger's home, or just a quiet moment to soak in some hot water and believe she'd be okay, she could have that.

He pulled out some soup base from earlier that week to heat on the stove while he brought most of the food into cold storage, pulling a few things to cook now. The non-perishable supplies could wait in the hallway until he got Jesra fed.

She finally emerged as he was testing the soup base, adding some more spices to help warm her up. He turned to tell her to make herself comfortable while he finished and froze at the sight of her.

Jesra was wearing one of his sweaters, which on her was like a giant oversized dress, and thick socks, and nothing else.

And he was totally unprepared for the bolt of lust that slammed through him and caused him to fully lose the power of speech.

Jesra had had a rough fucking day. Things were looking up—not, you know *good*, but not being drugged by slavers in the snow was definitely the right direction.

And the no-hesitation, lethal swordsman staring at her wide-eyed like someone had bopped him on the nose improved her mood even more than the shower had. She looked less like a bedraggled rat now, apparently.

"Thank you," Jesra said, crossing over to him as he swallowed, visibly shook his head once as if to clear it, and nodded at her impersonally.

Even better, a man who didn't expect to make his emotions her problem.

She wasn't quite sure she could make herself believe that.

"Your bathroom is awesome," Jesra added.

She'd never seen anything like it. No wonder he only had the one. The tub in there was practically big enough to be a pool, with multiple spray heads and even a small waterfall.

"Bathing in hot springs was common where I grew up in the Oruka Empire," Kazuron said.

The empire to the south. That matched his features—his skin had a golden undertone even though he inexplicably lived in the Frozen Wilds which weren't exactly known for their sunshine, eyes with epicanthic folds, and his starkly black hair over a face with such powerful lines she'd have known he was a warrior even without the sword.

"I live in the Frozen Wilds and have rich patrons; seemed worth the effort," he continued. "Do you have something against pants?"

Ha, still distracted then. Given that he didn't seem inclined to take it as an invitation, she didn't hate that.

"It may have escaped your notice, but you're not a small guy," Jesra said, in the understatement of the century.

The man had stripped off his outer layers, and she could see the bulge of his arm muscles, while his own pants clung to powerful thighs. How did someone so big move so damn fast?

When Kazuron snorted, Jesra continued, "Your pants are huge. I tried tying them on, but they kept slipping and I was tripping on the ends. So you'll have to cope with me pantsless."

It was ridiculous that she was pleased the extremely dangerous swordsman who was a stranger she was trapped with was taking note of her pantsless state.

She'd had a rough day; she could allow herself some internal ridiculousness.

"I'll muddle through somehow," Kazuron said dryly, "as long as you're not cold?"

"Firestarter," she reminded him. "I don't need them to keep warm."

"Ah, I wondered if that's why you weren't freezing." Kazuron nodded and continued stirring the giant pot and the stove as if she'd said nothing out of the ordinary, like she wasn't a freak of nature.

Then again, he apparently didn't exactly lead a bog-standard isolationist life. He'd known not to get sliced by the siliks' claws, and he'd known how to stay out of the way of a firestarter.

Fire elementals had once been common in the Frozen Wilds—back before they were frozen. Before each of the "protectates"—a frankly offensive name for them to give themselves, given that they were the ones who'd threatened the Wilds to begin with—had invaded to gain unilateral control of the intensely magical land at the heart of the surrounding mountains.

And the fire elemental population here had detonated it, and themselves, to keep those forces out.

Now, firestarters—descendants of those elementals, no matter how far removed—were a rare commodity. Little known, and less understood.

But the fire elementals of the Wilds had made sure everyone knew how dangerous they could be.

Jesra debated how much to tell the man who'd come to her aid—her instincts said she could trust him, but given the situation she'd just found herself in, fuck if those were working right.

But the point would become moot soon, and so far Kazuron had made an effort to be nothing but professional with her, so she said, "I'll probably crash soon. The slavers didn't provide anything to keep me warm, and firestarters run cold, so I'm a little low on power."

A *lot* low, but she wasn't going to admit *that*.

To distract him from that note, Jesra added, "We don't all have your enviable assets."

His eyebrows shot up. "I'm sorry?"

"Your natural ability to produce body heat, or so I assume, since you're not wearing long sleeves even in a *blizzard*."

Kazuron snorted, a smile curving his lips. "I thought you meant my giant tub."

And he had a sense of humor! Unfair.

"I'm standing in front of a magical stove," he added. "It's not *that* cold here."

Jesra huffed in amusement, unreasonably pleased she'd caught the joke and the smile out of him. Probably it had been too long since someone smiled at her without expectations, and wasn't that depressing?

It was a good reminder, though, that miraculous as he seemed, no one ever just gave her something for nothing. Not anymore.

But if they liked her, the price might be lower.

Jesra crossed the rest of the way to the stove. "Can I help?"

"Worried I'll poison you?" he asked.

She couldn't tell if he was serious or teasing. His dry humor was *really* dry, but in case he was actually offended, she said, "Trying not to be an overly burdensome guest. I could also use something to focus on to make sure I stay awake long enough to eat."

Kazuron looked sharply at her when she finished the first sentence.

Then he set the spoon down to make sure she knew she had his full attention.

His gaze speared through her, dark eyes piercing as surely as his blade. "You're not a burden," he said in a low, completely assured voice that made her shiver. "You don't need to earn being worth protecting."

It was only her years of practice with Galendon's court that kept her expression from completely shattering at that statement that came out of nowhere and hit her like he'd stabbed her in the heart.

A beat too long and she managed to get herself together enough to shrug, as if his words hadn't just flayed her, and broke their eye contact.

She'd had a rough day, she reminded herself again. She didn't have to judge her worth by a staring contest with a man who wanted to convince her she mattered.

It was just such a sudden, unexpected contrast to how she'd felt trying to justify her existence for years that now it caught off-balance.

That was all.

Jesra tried to joke to cover: "Do you say that to all your students too?"

It didn't work.

"Yes," Kazuron said, utterly serious. "I want them to wield themselves, not the other way around."

Another stab right to the heart.

Definitely no one had been trying to teach her that, Jesra thought bitterly. But she kept her voice as neutral and light as she could as she replied, "Then your students are lucky to have you."

His turn to shrug, turning back to the soup at last. "How successful I am as a teacher is a different question."

"Well," Jesra said dryly, past the lump that formed in her throat as she said the words aloud for the first time, "while I appreciate the sentiment, a colleague evidently decided my existence was such a burden he arranged to sell me into slavery."

Kazuron nodded, like this was a totally normal thing to talk about while making soup. "Untalented gentry?"

No stranger to that world, huh? "Talented, but not like me."

No one was talented like her. That was part of the problem.

"It's why I didn't expect it from him," Jesra found herself explaining. "I didn't think I was a threat to him."

Not that she could have done anything more about it. She'd already bent over backwards to appear unthreatening to everyone who should have been able to appreciate her talent—the other firestarters training at Eremor, the gentry who employed them. Short of dueling Bleic, who she'd always thought was too confident in his place to be bothered by her—which would have burned every possible political bridge and chance for her future—she couldn't have done anything about him.

Kazuron said, "So he was talented enough to never be sure he was shining as brightly as he should be in comparison, that being what he cared about. I know the type."

Got it in one. He was sharp. "Students of yours?" she asked.

"None I keep anymore. More so colleagues, before I retired. I learned. So have you."

Not that it would do her any good.

It was unlikely Bleic had managed this on his own—he wouldn't have known how to contact slavers. Galendon didn't even have those, or so she'd thought.

This swordsman might be dangerous in a physical fight, but nice as he seemed, with the political complications that were going to follow her, he might decide she was too much trouble.

She probably shouldn't point that out to him. But he was helping her, and he needed to be prepared, even if she didn't intend to be here for long. "The slavers will report that a swordsman in the Frozen Wilds got involved, and then they may come after you, too."

"Let them," Kazuron said, tremendously unconcerned, which sparked her irritation with him for the first time since he'd stopped her from chasing after their snowglider. "They'll find me a difficult target."

"You have to leave your cottage at some time," Jesra pointed out.

"They don't know where I live, and even if they find someone who can tell them, I'm a hard man to ambush," Kazuron said. "This is my ground, and they wouldn't be the first to think they could force me and surely won't be the last. The bigger problem is whether they'll come back for you."

Well, she'd tried. "They will. Lord Bleic wields too much influence at court, and the slavers will want payment—for their risk."

For their people, too? Maybe. She didn't know what slavers cared about. She resented mightily that she was being forced to find out.

"Where did they take you from?" Kazuron asked her.

She raised her eyebrows. "I'm a firestarter. You can't guess?"

"All five nations around the Frozen Wilds employ firestarters for any number of jobs, and I didn't find you on a normal path between any one of them."

Aw, he thought someone had dared employ her. Sweet of him.

"Eremor," she said. "I still live at the scholia in the palace."

They kept a fort right at the edge of their territory—in theory, to "defend" if any threats came from across the Frozen Wilds.

But mainly to keep the rest of Galendon's population safe from firestarters, because anyone who became a problem could be launched into the snow.

What she said hit her then, and she sucked in a breath. "I mean 'lived'."

Fuck.

Kazuron whistled low. "You do have a problem."

She didn't miss that use of the word 'you', and she didn't quite flinch.

"That narrows it down some where the slavers might have gotten to," he continued. "They might have had to take the long way around due to avalanches, so they could have been headed to one of the nearer villages in the Frozen Wilds, but it might also be somewhere unknown."

Jesra's shoulders drooped. So, she was safe for now, but she had nowhere to go back to and no idea how to go forward.

The soup spoon appeared in front of her. She blinked, looking up at him again.

"Just stir," Kazuron said.

Jesra took the spoon. She could do that.

She wondered if that's all he thought she was capable of, or if he was just trying to be nice, again, by giving her something to do that she couldn't mess up.

Glancing over at him, her eyes widened as she watched him start dicing vegetables like a goddamn artist.

How the fuck did anyone get that fast and precise with a knife that big? What in the hells!

After a minute of her staring open-mouthed, Kazuron noticed her expression and grinned—then immediately looked chagrined.

"Sorry, I'm good with blades," he said with a rueful smile. "You probably guessed."

Trying to lighten the mood, thinking he'd frightened her.

He was the first person who'd treated her like a human in longer than she could remember, and with an instant's clarity she realized she would not be able to cope if he decided she was easily breakable and had to be managed.

She would *not* have that from this man.

"I'd be worried," Jesra said, "if I couldn't set you on fire with a thought."

She raised her eyebrows calmly at him, as if to say that not only was she not intimidated by him, she didn't consider herself vulnerable, or less than equal, where he was concerned, either.

Kazuron eyed her speculatively for a moment, then nodded and continued dicing as if everything was just neatly settled, then.

Jesra let out a breath. Thank the gods.

"I'm allowed to be impressed at watching an artist work, surely," she said, as lightly as he had. "Is it all blades? Like, if you go out and chop firewood will I be in awe of your axe mastery?"

Kazuron snorted, hands never pausing. "Axes are different. It's swords and knives for me."

A horrible suspicion dawned on her. A lone swordsman who lived in the Frozen Wilds, who wasn't worried about anyone trying to attack him... and maybe actually had reason for that confidence.

Jesra said slowly, "And you're good enough to live like a hermit on your reputation."

"I am."

Shit, she was totally right. "Are you the Deathwind?"

Kazuron glanced at her as he chopped, wariness creeping into his tone now as he said, "I am."

Motherfucker. She'd been rescued by the fucking *Deathwind*, the most legendary swordsman of their age who still lived.

And maybe this was why he still lived.

But seriously, what were the goddamn odds? What was even happening in her life today?

Jesra felt giddiness bubbling up in her, and she recognized it clearly as relief.

Thank all the gods, for once in her life she'd stumbled onto someone who was too big a deal to need to use her.

She was going to crack after all, with hysterical laughter. "Are you sure I can't see your firewood-chopping technique? Maybe framed shirtless against the snow?"

After a shocked moment in which Jesra valiantly tried not to expire internally, sure her hysterics had gone too far, Kazuron's shoulders eased again.

Then his lips quirked.

"Are you sure you wouldn't rather give me a fiery backdrop?" he asked.

Her heart thumped.

The fucking *Deathwind* was playing with her.

Playing!

With *her*.

Jesra scoffed, "As if my tastes are so pedestrian."

The actual most dangerous swordsman alive huffed an actual laugh at that, dumping the vegetables into the pot.

In short order the soup was ready, which was good, because despite the new easy air between them Jesra was struggling to keep focused even on stirring the pot of soup. Only her determination to not fail at even this kept her eyes forced open.

She followed him to the table almost blindly, inhaled a bowl of soup, and even the Deathwind's legendary reflexes were barely fast enough to pull the empty bowl away as she slumped forward asleep, faceplanting into the table.

Jesra dragged herself slowly to consciousness, burrowed in warmth and heat directly against her skin—

She was so comfortable, and it had been so long since she awakened like this, it took her a moment to realize she *shouldn't* be warm.

Firestarters ran cold.

Until she woke enough to start heating herself on purpose.

She tensed, brain all at once kicking into consciousness fast enough to remember she was not at home and then to start taking in details like the fact that she was warm because there were strong arms wrapped around her, holding her while she slept, which was the *opposite* of professional—

But not as unprofessional as the hard erection pressed against her thigh.

"Are you awake now?" the most dangerous swordsman alive asked in a gruff voice.

"Why are you here?" Jesra asked tightly.

"I've been trying to disentangle myself so I can go pee," he said, tone very carefully even. "I need you to let go of me."

What?

Oh.

Oh, shit.

It wasn't until he pointed it out that she noticed she had a death grip on his shirt, her knuckles white and stiff. Jesra hissed as she quickly ran some warmth through them to loosen them up enough to let go.

Kazuron let out a quick breath of relief as he carefully extracted himself from her. She held very still against the drag of his cock and fought the urge to reach for him and his warmth.

Definitely just that.

Released from her hold, Kazuron was out the door in a flash, and Jesra buried her face in the blankets and groaned.

It wasn't him that had decided to make things weird; it was her subconscious.

She banged her head a few times as if she could retroactively knock some sense into it.

Well, so much for him seeing her favorably now, because she was officially the most awkward person in the universe.

And it was unfair for this to happen now that she was not only sure she liked him, but that she knew what his strong muscles—and erection—felt like, because she'd never get to appreciate them personally ever again.

Chapter 2

Kazuron returned quickly to the room as soon as he'd relieved the pressure enough to function in the same room as her.

Function *professionally*.

... And function not as a sex professional.

Gods, never mind, his brain was still hopeless.

But Kazuron snorted at seeing Jesra methodically banging her head against the blanket.

At least she wasn't panicking and fleeing into the snow after waking up in bed with her supposed rescuer. Chasing her down to prevent her from dying after the spectacle his penis had made of him this morning would have made an awkward situation even worse.

"I tried that myself," he told her from the doorway. "Let me know if it works any better for you."

She froze for a moment, then peeked up over the edge of the blanket.

Kazuron fought the smile trying to creep across his face even as his chest warmed.

Jesra was fierce, and she could and would kill her enemies without blinking.

And now he knew she could also be adorable. Maybe especially because of the rest.

Probably it would have been better for him not to know that.

"How did I get here?" Jesra asked tentatively. "Didn't you say there was a guest room?"

Hmm. Then again, the fact that she wasn't even accusing him might mean she felt like she couldn't do so safely without risking herself.

Well, he had come back to clear the air.

"There is, but it isn't heated yet, since I wasn't expecting guests," Kazuron explained. "I'd planned to put you in here and then go take the couch, but you wouldn't let go of me."

She winced. "Yeah. That, uh. Happens sometimes."

Kazuron blinked, his chest tightening abruptly. "What?"

"When I'm so low on magic that I can't keep myself warm," Jesra explained, "I'll attach myself to any heat source. I didn't realize I was in quite that bad of shape or I'd have warned you. I'm so sorry. Thank you for not freaking out."

He supposed it wouldn't have made sense for her to be unconsciously reaching for *him*.

Didn't mean his heart didn't fall a little bit at the extremely reasonable explanation, though.

"I'm so glad to learn I rate as a superior heat source to my blankets," he said dryly.

"Much superior," Jesra agreed, then blushed and covered her face with said blankets with a groan of dismay.

Kazuron barked a laugh, a sound that surprised him. But surely he still laughed?

But okay, not just a convenient heat source then. And she was willing to admit that out loud, so not only had he not scared her, he might have, somehow, made the right social move for once in his damn life.

It was definitely easier to find the situation amusing now that he'd peed and was sure she wasn't panicking.

And if Kazuron had really minded her clinging to him, he could have separated himself by force, which would occur to her eventually and then maybe he'd hide himself in the blankets too.

But he hadn't minded her fiercely clinging to him, not even a little, and *that* he really hadn't expected.

Kazuron had long since chosen loneliness over companions that couldn't meet his gaze, and knowing this woman was both attracted to him and could have *made* him leave without batting an eye if she wanted to was comforting in a way he hadn't realized he'd been missing—maybe because he'd stopped believing it was possible.

And not just comforting, but also a huge turn-on.

Not least because she hadn't put on any damn pants, and the awareness of how close she was to naked in his arms had not helped his morning situation in the slightest.

But that was his problem, not hers, and despite current evidence he could keep it to himself.

It wasn't like she was staying anyway, and he wasn't so desperate that he wanted pity sex from someone with no other options.

Kazuron's smile slid off. Well that had taken a turn. He shook his head and said, "I'll get some hot breakfast going. Feel free to bring the blankets."

She huffed. "Yes, you've got me, cocooned is my preferred way of interacting with the world."

A woman wrapped up in him and what was his was a kink he hadn't realized he had until she'd walked out of his bathroom yesterday, but every minute with her was reinforcing it.

Kazuron shrugged. "No judgment. If you don't want to expose yourself—to the cold—free of such a convenient shield, I have good aim."

Quick save, Kazuron.

"You're just going to throw food at my mouth like I'm a fish? I'll just try to swallow a whole breakfast sausage—"

Jesra broke off, face flushing beet-red, and Kazuron had no idea what to say as the image flashed through his mind of her waking him up by closing her mouth around his cock.

Finally Jesra said, "Please leave me to suffocate in your blankets in peace, or at the very least, have mercy and make me some tea. It may not be sufficient to solve my problems, but it can't possibly make them worse."

Kazuron laughed again, saluted, and left before *he* compounded their problems.

Or lost his damn mind and did something about them.

Jesra joined him a few minutes later, still rumpled in his sweater and socks, but she'd brushed her hair so it fell in soft waves around her face.

Kazuron felt vindicated in his decision not to torture them both with sausage and served her some heated-up leftover soup for breakfast instead.

"Thank you," she said, tucking her hair behind her ears. "Do you always cook this much at once, or are you expecting me to eat you out of house and home?"

Yesterday she'd put away more than he might've expected for someone her size, but he knew better than anyone that bodies needed fuel. He'd been relieved he hadn't had to talk her into it like some of his students.

"It's more that it's difficult to get a variety of supplies, since I don't often make the trek to the few villages in the Frozen Wilds. Easier to stock in bulk and cook something that'll last a while."

"Why can't you go more frequently? Are there blizzards that often?" Jesra looked toward the window and blinked for the first time. "Wow. That is a lot of snow, isn't it?"

"Nope. If it's not high enough that I can't open the door, it doesn't count."

She glanced at him. "That's a distressing way of measuring."

Kazuron grinned. "Not from snowy climes, huh?"

"Not at all," Jesra said. "It does snow in Eremor, but the palace employs people to make sure the roads are still accessible. So I've never had to really worry about snow, to be honest—it's just this novelty that looks pretty."

Novelty wore off fast. She wouldn't be staying long, Kazuron reminded himself. He didn't have to worry about what she thought about his home long-term. "Not like you have to worry about the cold, I suppose."

"Nope." Jesra grinned, and Kazuron somehow kept his expression even, despite how seeing her being mischievous warmed him all over, and despite the utter shock of the depth of his reaction to her. "Though the other students who grew up with snow always think I'm ridiculous, since I'm still happy to see it way past when they're ready to be done with it. Probably helps that I've never had to shovel it—and I wouldn't, either, since I can just melt a path in a pinch."

It doesn't matter. She's not staying.

His chest eased anyway.

"Though I guess you don't have to worry about roads out here," she mused. "So is it the blizzards? I'm not sure I've ever been in one before, now that I think of it. What's the difference between a blizzard and a snowstorm?"

"The next time you're awake through one, you'll know," Kazuron managed, like they were having a normal conversation and he wasn't experiencing an internal sea change.

Because that was all it could be, dammit, and he needed to remember that and not lose his mind and pressure her with whatever madness was taking him.

He continued, "We get the powerful storms from the magic backlash pretty regularly out here, but you usually have some warning when they're coming. And my snowglider can make it through one if I really need to."

"So, what then? You've had so much fine food in your day that you're fine boring your palate in retirement?"

Kazuron snorted. "Most of my life was not spent at court high tables."

"Sure, but once your reputation preceded you, you'd have spent some time there so the nobles could show you off like a prize pig, right? Or did they haze you with food instead?"

Her immediate understanding that being considered a highly valuable asset was not all it was cracked up to be persuaded him to risk answering honestly. "I don't do supply runs more often because my presence makes people uncomfortable."

Just his existence, which was better and worse than if it were personal. It wasn't like almost anyone around these parts knew "him" in any meaningful way.

They came here to escape threats, not have them shoved in their faces.

"Ahh. I can see that. Conversely, my status from official certification of firestarter training makes people *more* comfortable around me, since they don't think I'll set them on fire by accident."

So she'd completed her training then, but she still lived at the scholia rather than taking jobs.

Jesra said this lightly enough that he understood at least part of the problem. He hadn't moved to the middle of nowhere because he'd ever gotten comfortable managing what strangers expected from the weight of his reputation, after all.

Kazuron kept his tone as light as she had. "I would've thought they'd instead assume you could do it on purpose and get away with it."

"That would be true for gentry, but not me." Jesra stirred her soup. "Sometimes they think I'm getting above myself, but we all know if I slip up no one will bail me out. At least not for free, and I'm confident I wouldn't like the price."

Kazuron's eyebrows shot up. "You don't have a patron?"

Insanity. She'd demonstrated clear thinking even coming out of a drugged haze after being kidnapped and nearly frozen. Power aside, that level of judgment in battle conditions wasn't something you just left alone.

"Nope," Jesra said. "I'm not gentry, remember? So the patrons with interesting jobs won't touch me because I don't have connections, and the other offers I've received have been frankly offensive, given what I can do. I'm better off staying at the scholia rather than setting the expectation for my future standards with shitty work."

"Good for you," Kazuron said, and meant it. Hanging onto a sense of self-worth in her conditions wouldn't have been easy; enforcing it was even more impressive. "Never undersell yourself."

Jesra sighed. "Easier said than done. I knew I couldn't stay like that forever, but now I definitely can't go back but don't have anywhere else to go, either."

The words flew out of his mouth before his brain engaged. "You can stay here as long as you need."

An impulsive decision, and one that would probably torture him, but he meant it.

Jesra stared at him for a second, then nodded quickly, looking back down at her soup. "Thanks."

Of course she wasn't excited about whiling away her future alone in the snow with him. Couldn't blame her for that.

"Have you considered freelancing?" Kazuron asked.

"I don't have the money, reputation, or references to start on my own," Jesra explained. "I'd have to go mercenary. I don't think that's a life I could feel good about leading, because at least in the beginning I wouldn't have any say in the jobs I took."

Kazuron frowned. No disputing her conclusion, but he didn't like it. "If it comes to that, find me. I can make sure you get in with a better crew."

"Thanks," she said again, more warmly than before.

Ah, she'd thought it was a pity offer, and now she realized he was taking her seriously as a person with real skills to offer.

Kazuron nodded perfunctorily at her, one professional to another, and put some soup in his mouth so he didn't ruin the moment.

After a minute of silence punctuated only by the sounds of eating, Jesra asked, "So what do you do all day when you're not going on shopping sprees or cooking your body weight in soup or rescuing maidens not in distress?"

He glanced at her. "Maiden?"

She grinned. "Figuratively."

Oh thank the gods.

And the grin made him feel... playful.

"I'll show you," Kazuron told her.

Kazuron hadn't gotten a chance to show her the whole cottage last night since she'd passed out so quickly, so now he did.

Namely, the indoor practice room. Since she'd teased him about going shirtless in the snow, he stripped off his shirt for her and flexed while posing with a sword, not sure whether he was more pleased by the heat in her gaze or her laughter.

He very much didn't think about how long it had been since he'd made someone laugh like that.

After that, it was time to work through his morning exercises, and Jesra regrettably—if mercifully—didn't stay to watch, closing the door so he could focus.

Whatever else he was, Kazuron *was* a damn good swordsman, so focus he did, all his concentration on the simplest, most familiar exercises. A deadly kind of meditation, and he felt more clarity and calm for his efforts afterward.

It didn't last long when he emerged for lunch to see Jesra focusing on her own exercises.

Sitting alarmingly close to the fireplace in the main room with his wooden chess board in front of her, she focused a tiny spark of flame to limn one of the pawns—but not so closely it caught fire or even smoked.

What would that flame feel like on his skin?

That was a cursed thought, and now it wouldn't leave him as he watched, mesmerized.

Flame licked around the pawn, then vanished, like it was teasing. Once again, closer. Then again.

Then two pawns.

Kazuron's eyes widened.

That level of control was fucking unbelievable. With all he'd seen in half a dozen wars, *he* wouldn't have believed any firestarter could do that if he weren't watching it with his own eyes. He whistled, low and appreciative.

Jesra grinned absently. "When I run this low, it's best to start exercises back up with tiny amounts of power to reingrain discipline."

Back to extremely tight focus on the basics. Just like him.

"Should you not be resting?" Kazuron asked her.

"Nope. I don't know when the next attack will come, and I need to make sure I'm ready."

Couldn't argue with that. He'd protect her while she was with him, but she wouldn't want to rely on him and he respected that.

So he asked, "And the verdict?"

Jesra shrugged. "Not in optimal shape yet, but workable."

If that wasn't optimal, Kazuron hoped like hell he'd someday get to see what was. But he was almost as impressed with her professionalism—for someone who'd never taken a job outside school, she was not one to find herself unprepared.

Neither was he, but he wasn't sure how he could have prepared himself for her.

"I did take a break to make lunch earlier," Jesra said, letting all her flickers fade and getting to her feet. "I hope you don't mind. I made a *different* soup."

"A departure from my endlessly repetitive menu? How will I cope," he drawled.

Jesra grinned at him, and Kazuron found himself grinning back.

"I wasn't expecting cooking to be so nostalgic," she told him as she dished him up. "My grandpa used to love this in the winter, but I haven't had the chance to cook since I was little."

Kazuron's eyes flicked toward her. "Or see your family?"

Jesra paused; shrugged as she got settled at the table. "No. I didn't get the impression when they gave me up for firestarter training they had any interest in seeing me again. They could have sent messages at any time over the years. My grandpa probably isn't alive anymore."

And they hadn't bothered to tell her. Even if they thought she didn't care, that was harsh. Regretting bringing up a painful memory, Kazuron offered, "I didn't leave my family to seek out a life on the battlefield by accident. Some families don't deserve you."

Jesra glanced up at him, and their eyes met in perfect understanding.

Kazuron couldn't believe how easily they were getting along. Any time he accepted a student they always felt like they were underfoot, and any time he visited a village he felt like *he* was always in the way. If people walked down one side of the street and he tried to do the same, inevitably someone would walk the opposite direction and glare at him for doing it wrong—and then blanch and shuffle away once they realized who he was.

But here Jesra was, not interrupting his exercises and seemingly unbothered by his lifestyle, not to mention not intimidated by him. It was like everything he knew to be true about how he always was with other people was getting turned on its head, and the silence between them as they ate was… comfortable.

Until the explosion went off.

Chapter 3

Jesra was on her feet with fire wrapped around each fist in an instant.

"Easy," Kazuron said, though he'd risen too, and the casual Kazuron of this morning had vanished with his seat.

In his place was a man whose intensity was palpable. When he looked at her with those eyes, her heartrate accelerated.

And not for the right reasons.

"Heavy snow muffles sound," Kazuron murmured, "so I have traps set at a distance to warn of incoming intruders. You have enough time to get some pants on."

Jesra took a breath, glad he wasn't going to suggest she just hide inside—though he never had suggested she couldn't handle herself.

And his reminder about pants was probably a good one, since she was going to go outside. She'd flash-dry her pants and shoes from yesterday—it would be a little less heat she'd have to expend on herself.

"Clever," Jesra said, rolling out her shoulders. "So, time for the next round of fun already, then?"

He grinned at her briefly. "I'll go out first and try to draw them out, see if I can get them to tell me where they were taking you. If they're mercenaries, I might know them."

Jesra blinked and looked at him, realizing for the first time that he might have taken her from the slavers to not have to split a profit, but just didn't have his own buyer lined up and didn't know where to offload her either.

Kazuron paused, apparently catching her sudden doubt because he said, "Or not. Your call."

Gods, this man. He had about a million times as much experience as she did in a real battle and could kill a man faster than she could blink, and he would still defer to her to make sure she wasn't uncomfortable.

And maybe also because he believed she could handle herself. Unless that was a front, too.

But no. Jesra took a breath, remembering his instinctive reaction when he'd first seen her in the snow. This wasn't a long con. Kazuron was what he appeared to be.

Dangerous, yes, but only to her in a very specific way.

"I'm sorry," she squeezed out. "Being kidnapped is making me a little paranoid about my judgment."

Kazuron nodded, like that was the most natural thing in the world and not worth taking personally, which annoyingly made her feel even worse.

When was the last time she'd been able to make a mistake and not have it held against her?

"Understandable," he said, "but remember one mistake doesn't mean your entire judgment is worthless. I've seen enough to be sure of that. You ready for this?"

She was now, even if she had no idea what exactly he'd seen to make him so confident of her. "Yeah."

"I'll head out from the front. Come around from the back door when you're dressed."

"And then?"

The Deathwind shrugged his broad shoulders. "Depends on the situation."

"Improvise it is," Jesra said, walking away quickly. "I'm surprised you don't have a plan for that too."

"I have several, just not enough time to share them with you," he called after her tartly. She snickered despite herself. "We'll make it a priority later. But don't worry about me, just focus on what you need to do."

Jesra had no need to worry about him. Herself, yes. But not because of the slavers.

She dug her pants out of the laundry, grabbed her shoes, dried them out quickly and left some warmth for good measure as she slipped them on. They wouldn't be much protection from the snow, but some was better than none.

She didn't have to worry about Kazuron learning something he wouldn't share with her, either, because he'd done her the courtesy of yelling his conversation with them.

Unfortunately, everything from their end was high on threats and swear words and low on anything useful.

But there was a desperation she hadn't picked up on when she'd been kidnapped, and she wasn't sure what to make of it.

Questions for later. The slavers had been unprepared for him before, but not now. They wouldn't give anything away unless forced.

Jesra cracked her knuckles. She could go for applying some force.

She trudged out into the snow and almost immediately saw someone who'd come around the back. He saw her and fired an arrow.

Jesra lit it on fire before it could reach her chest.

She'd eaten and slept, and whatever state her judgment was in, there was nothing wrong with her reflexes.

Jesra was *so* happy to demonstrate why Bleic had had her drugged.

A shout from around the house—they'd heard the twang of the bow, probably.

Let them come.

Jesra shot a ball of fire from her hands at the bowman, but he dove out of the way.

Fine. She kept Kazuron's cottage behind her as she walked around the side, so no one could come up at her back.

The bowman shot at her again, and she got that arrow too. Another came from a different direction, and she also caught that one.

Jesra sent fireballs toward both the bowmen but slightly on the outside, driving them toward each other.

One froze, realizing she was herding them together so she could hit them.

And that was long enough for her fireball to land on him, sending him screaming and on fire to his death.

Just long enough for Kazuron to cut down the other, since she'd made it clear where he needed to go to intercept.

Across the snow, he mock-saluted her with his giant fucking sword, and Jesra grinned, blood soaring in a way she scarcely felt anymore.

This was what she'd been missing.

Oh, battle was part of it. She and Kazuron worked as a team: with strategic bursts of fire—she still wasn't at peak capacity, so she couldn't afford to just light everyone up—she herded the slavers to him, and he took them out.

The rush of getting to use her power for something she felt good about—she wasn't going to lose sleep over fewer slavers in the world, and certainly not ones after her—was part of it too, for sure.

Knowing someone competent that she trusted had her back, and trusted her to do her part competently in return... that was even headier.

And rare enough she wasn't sure she'd find it again if she left, or how long it would take.

No, not if. *When.*

As they wordlessly, inexorably fought through twenty goddamn slavers together before the last few managed to flee once more, she realized it was worse than that, because she liked Kazuron *specifically*. And it was unreasonable for her to want to stay with him when she'd known him for all of a day.

Jesra felt like she *fit* with him, though, and easily, and it had been so long—possibly ever—since she had fit anywhere.

But the Deathwind was retired. He didn't want the battle lifestyle anymore, and he hadn't signed up for her problems, even if he was making the best of it like a gentleman.

A gentleman who could wield a giant fucking sword and not falter no matter how many enemies he faced, which was so sexy she thought she'd combust.

So Jesra would cherish this interlude and take some memories of this time with her that she wouldn't regret.

And then she'd leave him to his hard-won peace.

When everyone around them was dead, having revealed nothing Jesra could use—even after their companions abandoned them, which she'd really thought would do it—she should have been frustrated that she still had no way forward into her future.

But when the world was silent and Kazuron strode up to her in the snow with his greatsword, her heart pounded, and she wasn't sorry.

Back inside, Kazuron immediately turned to Jesra and said, "Get your wet clothes off before you freeze. I'll get some pants to fit on you until we can get to a village to get you some of your own."

Jesra raised her eyebrows. "I won't freeze, but thank you."

"You were already low on power."

"Yes, but not *out*, which I believe I demonstrated."

"Your lips are blue," Kazuron growled.

"Are they?" Jesra shrugged. "Give me a minute."

She waved a hand and the fireplace flared to a blaze. Kazuron hurried to add more wood in case her magical fire didn't last to keep it going. By the time he turned around, she'd stripped out of her pants, shoes, and socks.

She was still too pale. He needed to warm her up before she could stand still half-naked.

Without a word he left to grab a pile of blankets from the closet, kicking his own snow-covered boots and socks off so he'd stop tracking icy water around the cottage and coming back to dump the blankets on the couch. "Sit," he told her.

"Where?" she asked, amused.

He wasn't. "Jesra."

She frowned at him but picked up a blanket and sat down, covering herself. "There. Are you happy?"

"No," Kazuron growled. He piled another blanket on her, making sure it reached all the way around so he could tuck it in, letting no cooler air inside her cocoon.

Jesra watched him with a strange look on her face. "Are you mad that we didn't manage to get any information out of even one of them?"

He'd gotten information from their dead bodies, which he'd share with her later once he was sure he wasn't falsely accusing innocent people. But at least some of those men had once been part of the Fanged Host, a mercenary band of siliks from Aksola that had leveraged their skills to make a life for their families out of the desert in fucking Rivnia.

Jesra was probably used to magical people in Eremor and wouldn't know that a mercenary band of *all* magical people—excepting that uncharacteristic asshole human whose head he'd sliced off when they first met—was rare.

The Fangs were solid, or they had been, which meant something had gone very badly wrong.

So he was mad about that.

But he was madder at how many of them there had been. He gritted his teeth. "I'm sorry I couldn't get anything concrete out of them."

"It's not your fault," Jesra said. "When you're outnumbered that badly, you have to prioritize, and not dying was more important than getting information. If their operation has enough people that they can spare a couple dozen to die in the snow, we should be able to find them, right? That's not a small cell."

Kazuron nodded tightly, adding another blanket.

Jesra huffed. "You're going to bury me, Kazuron. I'm fine."

"You are *not* fine," he growled.

"Okay, that's enough," Jesra said. "Go get something to drink and take a breath before I light you on fire. That'll warm me right up."

A drink. Yeah, he should have some water himself after all that exertion, and he could bring her something hot to help her warm up too.

When he put the kettle on, though, she sighed. "I don't need it heated, Kazuron."

"This will be better."

"Then I will heat it my own damn self. What the fuck has gotten into you? At what point in the middle of helping you fight off twenty slavers did you decide I'm incompetent, exactly?"

He bristled. "You're not incompetent."

"I'm well aware," Jesra snapped. "Do you think I've never been cold before? Do you think I'm incapable of taking care of myself?"

"I think you shouldn't have to," Kazuron said. "You're in my house, and you should—"

Let him take care of her. Know that she could depend on him. That she *deserved* to be taken care of.

But of course she couldn't depend on him, even if she was willing to, because he'd fucked up.

Jesra, thank all the gods, did not ask him to finish that sentence.

"So you're not mad about the slavers," she said slowly, "or at me. You're mad at yourself?"

"Of course I'm mad at myself," Kazuron growled. "The *first* thing I should have done today was make sure you had what you needed to take care of yourself and leave if you wanted. Boots. A fucking coat. It's inexcusable that I didn't, especially when we knew they were always going to come after you again."

Not to mention men he'd once fought with had turned slaver and he didn't know why, because he'd not only left them behind him, he'd shoved his damn head in the snow.

Instead, Kazuron had been relieved that Jesra hadn't wanted to leave him right away, and he'd been lulled into such a sense of cozy domesticity he'd let himself be distracted by it.

That was indefensible.

"Well," Jesra said, "I knew they'd come, but even I thought we'd have a little more time. Didn't you?"

"It doesn't matter."

"Okay, look. Come sit down."

"I'll be just a minute."

Jesra paused for just a moment and then said, very deliberately, "Kazuron. I sat down when you asked. Now it's your turn."

Fuck.

He turned off the kettle and about-faced on his heel to stomp back to the couch and then dropped down gingerly on the other side of it, not disturbing the blanket pile.

She reached out from behind the blankets anyway, and when he leaned forward with a wordless protest she slapped his hands away.

"Stop that. I'm fine. I understand why you're upset, and you're not totally wrong, but we are *both fine*. I am cold, and I am lower on power than I'd prefer, but I'm not going to pass out again. If another band of twenty slavers showed up right this second, I could take them.

So breathe, because if you're going to suffocate me, I will go steal your snowglider right this second and leave."

Kazuron sucked in a breath like she'd punched him. Suffocating her was the last thing he wanted. Even if he couldn't imagine asking someone who shone as brightly as she did to languish her talent out here alone with him, he wasn't ready for her to leave yet.

His second breath was shakier, but deeper. She was still here, and she wasn't mad at him, even though she should be. Or at least, she wasn't mad because he hadn't protected her the way he should have, but because he'd offended her sense of independence.

"I'm sorry," Kazuron said gruffly, leaving it as a blanket statement.

"Accepted," Jesra said, too easily. And then: "You know, if you really want to warm me up, you could use your natural abilities."

Kazuron snorted. *Because she still wanted to torture him.*

But to her surprise, and his, he did scoot over next to her.

And then scooped her and all her blankets up and sat her in his lap, her back against his chest.

She squeaked.

Kazuron went rigid beneath her. "I'm sorry, that was too far—"

He started to pick her up again to move her off, but Jesra grabbed his arms and pulled them around her middle, holding herself in place—to *him*.

"No, you're fine, you just startled me. I thought after this morning you'd have had enough of me."

"If I'd really wanted to get away," Kazuron said dryly, his voice low, "I could have made that happen."

Jesra shivered in his arms.

Kazuron didn't think it was from the cold.

His heart pounded.

"Oh?" Jesra asked lightly. "I know you wouldn't hurt me, though. So what were you going to use besides your brute strength?"

She knew he wouldn't hurt her.

Fierce possessiveness surged through him. Kazuron adjusted his grip on her, and before Jesra knew what he was doing he'd switched her position in a beat—so she was still in his lap, but now facing him, the blankets pooling around her middle.

Her eyes were wide, and she held on reflexively, but she didn't struggle or back away even a little.

She wasn't afraid of him. It was like a goddamn aphrodisiac. Kazuron began ever so slowly running his hands up and down her sides, warming her, watching her reaction like a hawk. The second she wanted to pull away, even if she didn't say anything, he would stop.

Jesra's hands tightened on his shoulders.

"I thought your specialty was blades," she said, her voice gone slightly breathy. "What's with the grappling techniques?"

Kazuron kept a lid on the satisfaction he felt at her tone, continuing to move his hands along her curves, with a little more pressure now. "When you fight with knives, it helps to know how the other person will move."

"And how," Jesra said in a sultry voice, "will I move?"

Kazuron's cock hardened in an instant, and that, finally, gave him pause.

So much for his goddamn professionalism. What kind of protector was he, exactly?

"I'm sorry," Kazuron said again, gruffly. "I got carried away."

"Did I object?" Jesra asked, irritation slipping into her tone.

No, she hadn't, but when she didn't have any option but to be here, taking advantage—

Jesra interrupted his train of thought. "Either I can trust my judgment or I can't, Kazuron, but you can't have it both ways. Which is it?"

Echoing his challenge to her before the battle, when he'd known perfectly well she was of sound enough mind to manage her power and composure in battle.

He was only doubting now because she wasn't afraid of him. But that was his issue, not hers.

Jesra was here, in his arms, and willing. Was he really going to stop now?

Tentatively, testing her reaction, he started moving his hands again. "I'm sorry," Kazuron said again. "How can I make it up to you?"

Jesra wrapped her arms more tightly around his neck. "Warm me up," she told him.

"I'll see what I can do," he said, his voice dropping lower. She shivered again, and Kazuron let a hint of smile peek out on his face at that.

He watched her as he slowly ran his hands up and down her sides, never looking away from her, both of their gazes locked on each other as the tension between them grew tauter with every moment.

Kazuron massaged circles into her flesh, which slowly—because Jesra's skin really was like ice—began to warm.

So he began to delve a little further.

Gauging her response, how she grew more pliant in his arms as she heated up, to gradually tightening as his hands began to delve a little further.

He stroked over her stomach, then a little lower until her breath hitched.

The undersides of her breasts, not quite grazing her nipples, as her breath turned shallow.

Down again, the gentlest of caresses over her mound.

"Kazuron," Jesra whispered.

The sound broke the spell.

Kazuron crushed his mouth to hers.

Her lips were cold, but not for long, the inside of her hot as he tasted her at last. He almost groaned with relief, with a fierceness for her he'd never felt before but that she was matching, matching *him*.

And as the heat of their kiss grew hotter with every stroke, his hands never stopped moving, touching her.

Finally Jesra pushed against his shoulders, gasping, and Kazuron went immediately, his own breath coming out harshly.

"Is that all you're going to do?" Jesra demanded.

He cocked an eyebrow, a playful smirk curving his lips as he clasped her to him. "And what are you going to do about it? I have you right where I want you."

It was absolutely a dare. He could hardly believe himself that he'd make a challenge like that, but before he could second-guess himself, Jesra's expression arrested him.

That was not the face of a woman who felt threatened.

Now it was his turn to shiver.

"What will I do?" Jesra asked rhetorically.

Then she lit a tiny spark of flame on the tip of her pointer finger and pointed it at his chest.

Hardly daring to breathe, Kazuron lowered himself down the couch, away from the fire as it followed him, close but not too close. Just like the goddamn chess piece.

Now he was her pawn.

"What will I do?" she asked again, and when his back was against the couch, Jesra scooted forward, positioning herself right on top of his cock.

So she could feel it hardening beneath her as she stroked that tiny little spark of fire down the center of his shirt, parting it like a knife through butter, without lighting anything else on fire. Just the tease of the heat against his skin.

Jesra tore his shirt apart and put her hands on him, and Kazuron's breath hissed out between his teeth.

Her hands were hot, not burning like fire, but almost sparking against his flesh, and every single one of his nerves leapt to attention.

Jesra scooted back further and he almost groaned as her pressure left him.

But then she yanked his pants down, rising up just for an instant as he lifted his hips to help, and she took the opportunity to throw off the rest of the blankets and the sweater she was wearing, too.

Kazuron's breath caught at the sight of her, naked to his gaze and on top of him, bold as you please, the most erotic thing he'd seen in his life. But when he reached for her, she pushed his hand away and sat down on his legs, the tiny flame on the finger of her other hand once again lit at the tip.

Which she slowly, eyes never leaving his, lowered to his cock.

Kazuron stilled completely, so turned on he couldn't even breathe.

Then Jesra used that fingertip to draw a ring around the base of him and circle him in flame.

Not burning him, because her control was unreal, but licking him with heat.

Then that ring of fire began stroking up and down his length, and Kazuron had never been this hard in his goddamn life, already leaking at the tip as he struggled to hold himself perfectly still for her, and she hadn't even touched him yet.

"What will I do?" Jesra purred a third time, and his cock *twitched*.

Soft flame coated her hand, and Jesra ran it up and down his length.

Kazuron practically arched out of his body with a yell.

When he dropped back down, panting, she had the audacity to *grin* at him, not even a little worried and knowing full well what she was doing to him, and that was before she bent down and gently sucked the tip of him.

Kazuron swore, scrabbling at the couch for purchase as her hot mouth closed more fully over him, those flickering flames at his base still teasing him, and before he could explode in her mouth, with an effort of will he reached down and hauled her up by the shoulders.

"Let me touch you," he growled.

"You had your chance," Jesra informed him archly.

The hells he had. Kazuron reached down between them and circled her clit, a quick tease, and then slipped a finger inside her.

She was hot—of course she was hot, she was a firestarter, but she was *ready* for him, open and already so wet he slipped a second finger inside her immediately.

Her inner walls clamped around him as she let out an almost mewling sound, and Kazuron wanted nothing so much as to hear that again.

"There's one place," he said, his large fingers filling her, "that I haven't had a chance to touch yet. Allow me to correct that."

Jesra's head fell back as he stroked inside her once, twice, and on the third time she moaned, grinding down on his fingers.

With a sharp breath, she abruptly lifted herself off him and said, her voice shaky, "I think you've misunderstood. I'm the one who has *you* where I want you."

She grabbed his shaft with fire around her hand, and then in a single move she slid down over him.

They both groaned.

"Wait—" Kazuron barely managed in a strangled voice, lifting his head.

"I have a pregnancy ward," Jesra said quickly.

He flopped back down on the couch. "Oh thank the gods."

Jesra snickered, even that much movement shifting them, and their breaths caught again.

Then Jesra grinned down at him evilly. "Now *I*," she said, "am going to ride *you*."

Kazuron did not have a single damn objection to that whatsoever and stayed right where he'd been put.

But he wasn't going to be passive anymore.

Jesra bent over him to deepen the angle, moaning as he hit the right spot inside her. Kazuron memorized the angle as he stroked over it again and again and matched her rhythm.

Then he raised himself up on his elbows and took one of her breasts in his mouth, massaging the other with a hand before pinching her nipple.

Jesra gasped, and then she slid sparking hands up his chest, and Kazuron bucked against her.

And then he nipped at her breast.

Jesra shuddered over him, and Kazuron continued lapping at her breasts, oh-so-gently, teasing her to a frenzy.

And then he bit her again on the other side.

Jesra's orgasm caught her suddenly, and Kazuron continued stroking her through it, in and out, in and out, until she finally slowed.

And then in another quick move, he flipped them on the couch.

Jesra was still catching her breath as he lifted one of her legs, and she wrapped the other around him, hips falling wide as she reached up and touched his face like she was afraid she'd break him.

No one had been afraid of *that* in a long damn time.

No one had believed he should be treated as if he could be, either, and the tenderness in her, for him, almost undid him.

But instead he lifted her leg higher, twisting her slightly, and Jesra gasped as he corkscrewed into her at an even deeper angle.

She moaned, an utterly wanton sound that made him smile with satisfaction and do it again, and again, twisting into her and stroking every part of her on the inside.

But even now she was unwilling to just lie back and let him pleasure her, because Kazuron could feel that fire licking around the base of him again, then tightening, with just a touch of pressure.

And then her fire *pulsed*.

Kazuron actually stopped breathing for a moment, losing his rhythm as his mind went utterly white with pleasure.

And then he was coming harder than he'd ever come in his life, driving into her relentlessly as her cries matched his in fervor, and her second orgasm—thank the gods—crashed through her, chasing his.

For a minute he just knelt above her, breath heaving, staring into her eyes in a profound kind of shock, comforted that her expression echoed the feeling back at him before a slow smile stole across her face.

He felt it on his own, too, something like giddiness overtaking him.

Kazuron's arms of all things were still shaking as he finally slipped out of her, grabbing a blanket off the ground and using it to wipe them both up in broad strokes, a blanket not really being the right tool for the job.

Then with the last of his strength he flipped them one last time so he wouldn't crush her. Jesra crawled up his body and kissed him again with aching sweetness, and Kazuron wrapped his arms around her, holding her close.

They stayed like that for a long time, both of them quiet, processing the world reorienting itself on a different axis.

He was, at least, and he hoped like hell she was too, that he wasn't alone in this, but he didn't know the words to ask.

Kazuron couldn't remember the last time he'd felt this peaceful, this *sure*.

It was like the sense of rightness knowing he was fighting for the correct cause, the same sense he'd had when he left it all behind him once and for all, and now, he felt it with her.

Finally, Jesra said, "I don't know where to go from here."

Kazuron's heart clenched, and he kissed the top of her head. "I have some ideas."

Jesra huffed in amusement and wiggled against him. He grinned, but understood she didn't mean just their relationship, but her future.

So he said, "You don't have to decide your entire future all at once. You have time, and options."

"Do I?" she wondered aloud. "I wasn't expecting them back so soon, which makes me think there may not be that much time before they plan to move. And if they're moving—"

"They're probably moving other people too. I know. We'll go into town and see what we can find out tomorrow."

A pause. "I thought you didn't want to deal with people more than necessary."

Did she think he'd just lend her his snowglider and wave her on her merry way while he stayed behind and watched her go? "I don't enjoy watching them be afraid of me, but this is more important. I can help with that much, at least."

And more if she wanted. If she'd let him. But that was up to her.

Softly, Jesra said, "Thank you."

And in that Kazuron heard all the things she thought she needed to thank him for, so he didn't say "you're welcome."

It was unreasonable for him to feel so desperate for her to choose him after a single day, and he wouldn't ask her to. So he just tightened his arms around her and said, "You're here now."

She didn't fight his hold, but she also didn't answer.

After a minute, she gently pulled back, extracting herself from him so much more deftly than he'd managed this morning, and left.

Kazuron swore his heart left with her.

He was a mess. He could hear her going to the bathroom. It wasn't like she was even *gone* gone.

He shoved a fist between his eyes. Gods, what a *stupid* thing to say—

But then Jesra was back, with wet cloths, and she cleaned him up more thoroughly, endlessly gentle, while Kazuron watched her with his heart in his throat, not daring to speak again.

Then she drew another blanket up and laid down over him again, and echoed him like a prayer, "I'm here now."

Kazuron had the terrifying thought that he might fall to pieces right beneath her and breathed deeply, evening his breath through long practice as he settled his arms back around her, his hammering heart slowly calming once more with her warmth pressing into him.

Eventually he realized that her even breathing meant she'd fallen asleep on top of him, all barriers down between them.

Kazuron held still, holding onto that precious tender feeling for a long time, until sleep finally claimed him too.

Chapter 4

They got a late start the next morning. When Kazuron had finally been forced to leave Jesra's arms to answer the call of nature, he arranged her, cocooned in blankets, by the fire and got to work at what he should have done the day before.

First, improvising some straps to add to a pair of his pants so they'd actually stay on her. Digging out a pair of boots she could stuff with socks. Dusting off his old coat so she could wear his good one.

She'd hardly be at the peak of fashion, and it would be a little awkward to wear, but she wouldn't have to waste power to prevent herself from freezing, either, whenever she had to go.

He wanted her to stay, which was absolutely unreasonable; Jesra had her whole life ahead of her. And she deserved to both have options and *know* she had options.

If she stayed with him out of desperation, or worse, pity, one day it would all come apart and Kazuron knew himself well enough to know how hard that would hit him. He'd gotten in too deep, too fast.

So fighting his desire to smother her in himself the whole way, he got a bright-eyed Jesra dwarfed in his coat and tragically wearing his rolled-up pants—clomping around in his too-big boots with such unabashed hilarity his heart squeezed—loaded into the snowglider and on their way to the town of Driftfall.

Where he would have to, for his sins, talk with people.

He tried to convince himself that it was worth it, because Jesra did need boots that fit if she was going to go anywhere—*or* stay.

"Oooh, let me try driving," Jesra said.

"You don't even know where you're going," Kazuron said, amused.

Jesra went abruptly tense beside him, and Kazuron silently cursed himself. That phrasing would hit a little too close to home for her.

Their easy banter from before had probably been a fluke, and it was better for them both to know that now. He never knew how to talk about anything but swords.

Still, he would try to fix this.

He wasn't ready to lose her yet.

Kazuron said, "I can show you how to drive on the way back."

"I don't need you to be my teacher."

Damn it, she *was* mad. "Good, because I'm not interested in being your teacher," he said. "I can just imagine assigning you exercises and you burning off my pants instead."

That got the tiniest smile out of her, and Kazuron went practically giddy with relief.

Storms, he had it bad.

"Exercises, is it," Jesra teased.

Kazuron nodded firmly. "Exercises, absolutely. Good for health."

"If you couldn't focus when I wasn't wearing pants, then maybe you're the one who needs more practice."

"Never can have enough practice."

"That's true," Jesra mused. "Though I'll have you know I was a very diligent student."

Then she went quiet again.

He was pretty sure he wasn't the problem this time.

"How fortunate for me, then," Kazuron said, "that you don't need a teacher now."

Jesra didn't answer, her gaze on the expanse of snow before him. Kazuron kept his mouth shut and tried not to take it as a rejection.

But after a few minutes, she didn't speak up again.

The whole point of this trip was for Jesra to believe she had a future that wasn't mired in her past, so Kazuron girded his damn loins and tried again.

Maybe business would work where personal connection hadn't.

"Driftfall isn't the biggest town in the Frozen Wilds, but it's the closest to where I live," he said.

On Rivnia's side of the Frozen Wilds, too, which wasn't an accident. Rivnia didn't have a great track record where magical people were concerned, and sometimes those people opted out.

Desperation was the reason anyone came to the Frozen Wilds.

Even, Kazuron suspected, the Fanged Host.

"The tavern keeper, Hansul," he added, "he's sharp."

That got her. "You think he might know something about the slavers?"

"Not directly. I can't see him abiding that kind of thing, and I haven't noticed anything different in his manner lately. But he's better positioned to find something out."

"So, he's not going to just point me down the street so I can take care of this today," Jesra said wryly, but there was a note of weariness in her voice. She was looking down a long, empty future she couldn't even start to shape until she had this behind her.

Whereas she'd crashed into the emptiness in his life, and Kazuron had a feeling she'd already changed it irrevocably.

"Probably not," he said, "but he might also know if there's any work to be had for firestarters."

Jesra raised her eyebrows at him sardonically. "Oh? Like what?"

Kazuron opened his mouth, closed it again.

Not anything she'd be excited about. She'd already turned down plenty of work that wouldn't challenge her.

Kazuron so badly wanted to have real hope to offer her, but he wouldn't lie to her. She'd had more than enough of that.

"Not much worth your skills," he finally said. "It could be a way to start making money of your own and building references and reputation for competence. But not anything you'd want to do long-term."

Nothing that would persuade her to stay.

Jesra nodded. "So what all do they have in Driftfall?"

Kazuron blinked at her.

"Good food?" she prompted. "Music gatherings, maybe? Why do people live there?"

He didn't have any goddamn idea. No one fled to the Frozen Wilds unless they felt they had no other options—and that was maybe hitting a little close to home for *him* today—but he didn't know their personal stories.

Kazuron didn't socialize; he stocked up on supplies and got out. *He* was out here to keep out of the Five Protectates' business, not get involved.

But here he was, involving himself. Damn it.

He cast desperately around, trying to think of anything he might have heard from Hansul about a local festivity, until Jesra snorted and patted him on the shoulder.

"Don't strain yourself, you misanthrope," she told him dryly.

Kazuron scowled. "I don't hate people."

"No, just interacting with them in any way. Very different." Her expression was teasing, which Kazuron decided was an improvement, even if it was at his expense.

But to his relief, she didn't poke any more fun at him about it nor try to convince him he was wrong about how people saw him, either. He'd been worried she would pity him, but he shouldn't have.

She would understand what it was like for people to always perceive you as a threat.

Her actions when they got to town, though, were very different than his approach.

Kazuron started out leading her to the tailor's shop. A bell tinkled above the door, and a slight girl with green skin and bright pink hair blanched before greeting them nervously.

"Welcome to The Clever Cloak! How can I help you today?"

Kazuron pointed at Jesra. "She needs clothes that fit. Clothes fit for the Frozen Wilds."

Jesra frowned up at him. "I do have clothes."

"Not right now, you don't."

She raised her eyebrows and looked herself up and down. "Oh? Are these pants an illusion? I can't see why we bothered wearing them then. I'm sure the town would appreciate the view of you pantsless."

The shop girl choked. "I'll just... get Entaru," she squeaked before dashing into the back room.

Kazuron leveled a look at Jesra.

She grinned up at him unrepentantly. "Well, Kazuron? Do you really think I need more pants?"

Not if she never left his bed she didn't.

"If you don't want to wear them later, I certainly won't force the issue," he said, his voice lower than he'd intended. "But if you don't want to go back to Eremor to retrieve any of your old ones, you won't have to."

Jesra studied him thoughtfully.

Then Entaru, a knobbly and impeccably neat man—no small feat out here; it might have had something to do with whatever he could shape-change into—came out of the back with the shop girl trailing wide-eyed behind.

No species divisions in the Frozen Wilds. It was one of the few things Kazuron *did* like about the villages here.

Entaru's hands were clasped tightly in front of him so they wouldn't shake, but otherwise his expression gave nothing of his discomfort away.

"Kazuron-zana." Entaru bowed stiffly, and Kazuron's eye twitched at the address, as if he were a nobleman. "I hope you've been well."

"Entaru-koro, likewise," Kazuron said briskly, adopting a respectful but much more common form. "This is Jesra. She's been unfortunately separated from her belongings and needs some clothes."

Entaru's gaze turned to Jesra, and his expression froze.

Then Jesra smiled in a way he'd never seen from her, spreading her arms wide. "I'm sure you can't see why. Kazuron obviously has a secondary career ahead of him as a tailor, and pants so big they drag on the floor will be all the rage next season." She arched an eyebrow at Kazuron. "All your pants are custom-made, aren't they? Do normal humans even come in your size?"

"Not commonly," he said dryly.

"Well, there you go then. I need some more normal-human-sized pants, ideally that I won't trip over. And a coat, so Kazuron can have this one back. His arms are likely to burst the seams of his old one there, which seems like a cruel thing to do to it."

Entaru let out a breath. "I'd be delighted to help, Jesra-zana—"

"Oh, just Jesra, I'm not noble or anything." She glanced back at Kazuron. "Wait, are you?"

Depending on who you asked and which war he'd been serving in, that was complicated. But Kazuron said, "No."

He was a little surprised Jesra understood the nuances of the honorifics, given that she'd never left Galendon. Their use was common in the Oruka Empire and the eastern protectates, but not in the west. And in Eremor she would have been insulated from much of international politics.

"Ah, that's why your eye did that thing," she said. "Kazuron-koro it is, then. Or maybe I'll go with Kazuron-ten."

Jesra winked at him at the notion of applying such an informal marker to him, one that implied closeness—and gods, when was the last time anyone had been close enough to him to call him that without being patronizing?—and then peered around Entaru. "And I didn't catch your name?"

The shop girl's name, it turned out, was Fumiye, and she was more than happy to chat with Jesra about the fabrics they had available while Entaru took her measurements.

And while Kazuron reeled at Jesra's abrupt charm offensive. He'd never seen her around people that weren't trying to kill her, and he was totally unprepared for how much charisma she could activate when not half-frozen—or taking charge of his cock.

But she didn't turn the charisma only on Fumiye and Entaru. Jesra modeled her new clothes for *him*, asking Kazuron's opinion only to quip back at him, drawing dry answers out of him as her comments grew increasingly ridiculous and he was unable to hide his amusement.

And their interactions amused Fumiye and Entaru, too, as they relaxed around him, and that, Kazuron realized, had been Jesra's goal all along.

Her obvious recognition that he was different but without deferring to him in any way made them look at him differently, too.

By the time they left, Fumiye had secured a promise from Jesra to visit again the next time she came to town, and Kazuron ached at the beat of hesitation before Jesra warmly agreed.

The bell tinkled again as the door shut behind him.

"Well," Kazuron said, carrying a bag of her clothing. "That was certainly an experience."

"Performative extroversion," Jesra agreed lightly. "Making anyone feel like we're friendly has its uses."

A front she'd learned to wear to smooth her way in circles where she was an outsider. To feel like, but not actually be, friends.

She must have been lonely, too.

"Not a skill I learned," Kazuron said dryly as he led them to the tavern. "In my younger days appearing dangerous was the best way to survive."

"*Not* appearing dangerous can actually work just as well."

"Personal experience of both?"

Jesra looked thoughtful. "It's possible that was a flaw with my strategy, actually. I never really was deferential."

"That's their problem."

"I mean, it's literally mine, but I appreciate the support." She patted him on the shoulder again.

Kazuron snorted as he pushed open the door to the tavern.

So Hansul's first view of him was a shopping bag, an amused expression, and company not intimidated by him.

The tavern keeper's bushy eyebrows shot all the way up.

Kazuron glanced back at Jesra.

She winked at him again.

He fought a smile even as he rolled his eyes. Of course she'd planned that, his devious little firestarter.

No, not his. *Stop that, Kazuron.*

"Welcome to The Toasty Taphouse," Hansul said, drying glassware like early afternoon was a normal time for anyone, and Kazuron most of all, to drop by. "Who's your new friend, Kazuron?"

"Jesra," she answered him warmly—probably because he'd used Kazuron's name plainly. "You look like you've never seen him smile before."

"Can't say that I have," Hansul agreed, yellow eyes glowing amused against his dark red skin and horns.

Hansul was average size for an orun, but that was still plenty big enough that he wasn't easy for humans and smaller races to intimidate. It gave him an easy confidence that made him more comfortable dealing with Kazuron than most people.

"Well, maybe you need to workshop some jokes," Jesra said as she crossed the room and seated herself in front of him on a bar stool. "Isn't that why you run a tavern, to nourish the people?"

"On the contrary," Hansul said smoothly in his rumbly voice, gesturing at Kazuron, "it's for the quality of the company."

Jesra burst out laughing and said to Kazuron, "Never mind, it's definitely you that's the problem."

Kazuron rolled his eyes again. But he also realized she was trying to facilitate an easier relationship with a man he respected—he'd told her that, after all— so he made an effort to participate in kind.

"Don't let him fool you," he told her. "Hansul has a finger in every shipment that comes to this place and can turn a profit from anything."

Hansul paused in wiping a glass. "Are you unhappy with my prices?"

Why was he so bad at this? One sentence and he'd misstepped. He didn't have Jesra's deftness at conversation to fix it easily either. So Kazuron just said directly, "No, I can afford what you charge me."

Hansul picked up again as if their banter hadn't stuttered to an uneasy halt. "In that case, I have a crate of frozen fruit that was misdelivered. If you're in mind for a treat."

That *was* a treat. Fruit was rare in the Frozen Wilds.

But that wasn't why Hansul had offered it to him, and he tried to seize the branch extended.

Kazuron blew out a breath. "I'd better, at the rate Jesra's going through my stores."

"Well, if you want to keep me out of them, I can be satisfied," Jesra suggested with an eyebrow waggle, "with baked goods." She winked at Hansul. "As long as we're upselling him here."

"Hard to keep those fresh, if you're planning on being around for a while," Hansul probed.

Jesra smiled. "Easier if you can magically remove the heat and add it back when needed."

The tavern keeper blinked. "A firestarter?"

Kazuron watched him consider Jesra anew, because he knew enough of the world to recognize the kind of control she implied casually wasn't common.

And then Hansul glanced back at Kazuron and asked, "You taking a job?"

Kazuron's chest tightened. Hansul was sharp. Even he recognized firestarting skills at the level Jesra had just implied were meant for bigger things than rotting in the middle of nowhere and assumed the only reason she'd be with him is if he had something big to offer her.

For the first time, he was beginning to wish he hadn't become such a recluse that he actually could.

But before he could answer Hansul, Jesra jumped in and said, "No, he's just taking pity on a poor unfortunate. You know what he's like."

Hansul glanced back at her and said dryly, "I have a notion. So are you going to need another supply order, then?"

Kazuron blinked at him, startled that Hansul of all people assumed that his recalcitrant self was going to help and that it wasn't a strange position for him.

Maybe Jesra could drive everyone mad, and not just him.

"Could be," Kazuron managed as casually as he could, not wanting to pressure Jesra by speaking for her future plans.

Hansul eyed him and nodded knowingly, and Kazuron realized the tavern keeper had seen even more than he'd meant him to.

He cleared his throat. "Aside from Jesra's apparent penchant for dessert—"

"Oh, I'll take bread too. I'm equal opportunity with baked goods."

Without missing a beat, Hansul withdrew a warm loaf of bread from behind the bar and passed it over to her. "On the house."

Jesra broke into a smile. "The *Toasty* Taphouse! I love it."

Hansul's lips twitched, and Jesra tore into the bread with delight.

Kazuron's chest ached at the sight of her so plainly happy from something so very simple.

And then he noticed Hansul watching him knowingly again, and understood he'd gotten the bread out as a friendly gesture for *Kazuron.*

He rolled his eyes again, though with a wry smile at how apparently easy he was to read.

"Next time I come, better add a cake to my order," he told Hansul dryly.

Hansul's eyes laughed at him. "Pleasure doing business with you as always."

And that was his cue. "I have a different kind of business to ask about, if you can say."

Hansul's eyes narrowed a fraction, but Jesra nodded sagely. "Ah, that's it, you're really in the tavern business for all the hot gossip, aren't you?"

She *was* good, taking the sting out of his awkward question.

Hansul flashed a quick, appreciative grin at her before raising his eyebrows in Kazuron's direction. "What can I help you with?"

"Not sure you can," Kazuron said to get things started. "But it's come to my attention that slavers are operating in the Frozen Wilds."

Hansul's eyes widened. "*What?*"

He hadn't really expected Hansul to be involved in covering their tracks, but his obvious shock was still a relief. "Took me by damn surprise too," Kazuron told him.

"I know you wouldn't say that if you weren't sure, but with you known to live out here, I can't believe they'd dare," Hansul said.

Kazuron blinked, momentarily derailed. "I haven't lifted a finger for that sort of thing in years."

"Don't have to," Hansul said. "Everyone knows you could."

Kazuron wasn't sure what to make of that.

Jesra had no such dilemma. "In this case I have reason to believe they are being heavily financed to make it worth their while."

Hansul regarded her. "Are they, now."

She took another bite of bread, matching the tavernkeeper's stare.

Kazuron felt a surge of affection for her. She wouldn't defer to anyone.

Finally, Hansul said, "They're not here. And I wouldn't break bread with them if they were."

The tavernkeeper wasn't going to sell her to slavers, even with what they'd revealed to him.

Jesra forced her shoulders to relax, relieved she—and Kazuron—hadn't misread him. It would take her nerves a little while longer to settle.

Kazuron interrupted mildly, "Didn't think they'd be here, or you'd have said something when I picked up my last order."

Hansul glanced sharply at him, then back at Jesra, and she watched the dawning understanding that Kazuron *would* do something about a situation like this if he knew.

The tavernkeeper nodded slowly, and Kazuron continued, "So I thought, given how closely you watch everything coming into town here, you might have an idea if anything has changed recently elsewhere in the Frozen Wilds. Someone who has more money than you'd expect. Someone who's gone quiet. That sort of thing."

Hansul stiffened before Kazuron had even finished. "Now that you mention it, yes, but it never occurred to me that might be the reason. Thought since we've had a rough patch of storms lately that Rimepeak might have just had some extra trouble, either less excess to trade or the town snowglider died. But I haven't heard anything from them for a few weeks now. Not long enough that I was worried, since all of us out here plan in order to hold out at least a couple months if things get bad, and Nomin's sharp, but... goddamn it."

"Don't blame yourself," Kazuron said. "It makes sense the slavers wouldn't have been there long. Probably Rimepeak didn't know what the slavers were up to when they were scouting, then they planned to get in and out before anyone realized what was up."

Kazuron had dealt with slavers before.

It ought to have been comforting that at least one of them knew what they were doing, but Jesra's stomach dropped at the reminder of just how much more experienced he was.

She'd never even driven a goddamn snowglider.

And without his help, it wouldn't matter how skilled of a firestarter she was, or how good at managing at court. She'd never catch the slavers on her own.

The feeling had been building for a long time now, but her experiences the last few days had brought it to a head:

Jesra was *very* tired of not being able to control her own life.

And since the strategy she'd put everything into had exploded in her face, it was time to figure out how to change that.

Hansul asked skeptically, "You think slavers would bother to set up for a few weeks for a one-time gig?"

Kazuron hesitated. "No. Probably they were planning to set up for a recurring pipeline."

"Which means this might also not be the first time," Hansul pointed out. "Rimepeak's gone dark before, the last couple years. You didn't know?"

Kazuron frowned. "I noticed when they stopped supplying me a couple years back, but I thought..." He looked down, jaw working, and didn't finish the sentence.

But he didn't need to. He'd thought it was him that made them uncomfortable, and he hadn't pushed. And all the while if he had, he might have been able to rescue them from slavers.

Jesra wanted to distract him from guilting himself, and it was pretty damn easy, given how her own anger at this whole situation was rising.

"So you're saying," she said, "that a band of slavers has slowly taken over a town so they can't ask anyone for help, or at least feel they can't lest they be judged as accomplices. Do you think they are helping the slavers?"

"Not willingly." Hansul shook his head. "They're good people there. There's always someone looking for a quick score, but if the slavers are having any success, more than one or two people would have to be involved and I can't see Rimepeak's people agreeing. Not by choice."

"It can be less risky," Jesra said softly, "to not make a dangerous choice. Especially if you think no one will help."

Kazuron glanced at her sharply.

She ignored him.

Hansul said flatly, "Not for something like this. We may be poor compared to what you're used to, but that doesn't make us bad people."

"My family isn't gentry, but they weren't poor. They still sold me."

"I'm sorry to hear that," Hansul said. "It doesn't mean we would."

Jesra shook her head. "That's not what I mean. My family thought they were helping me, and it's true I never could have gotten the training I needed with them. Could it be something like that?"

For the first time since they'd brought up slavers, Hansul's expression softened. *Pity.*

And it wasn't knowing she'd been kidnapped that brought that out of him.

Jesra's chest burned.

Too gently, Kazuron said, "Rimepeak wouldn't be hiding it if it were something like that."

Right, so she was too innocent of the world to have realized all the implications immediately, and now they thought she was a child. Awesome.

Jesra shrugged like she'd just been covering options, and hadn't she? "Okay. So the slavers have taken over the town somehow. Or—is everyone involved in shipping? Is it possible not everyone in town knows? "

Mercifully, Hansul answered the new question without further comment. "No. Out here, in the winter storms' high season, we live and die by our connections. Even someone who isn't involved in shipping will talk to those that are."

"Hostages, then? Or threatening to enslave anyone who protests?"

"No. People would have banded together."

"There are a lot of mercenaries," Jesra pointed out, getting a little annoyed he kept shooting down everything she offered without presenting an alternative theory. "Though that might be new."

"It doesn't matter," Kazuron said, and Jesra gritted her teeth. "The mercenaries aren't the ones who handle the plumbing or growing of food. They can't threaten to salt the fields if they plan to return."

Jesra kept her tone even. "If they decide the town is too much trouble, they could do it on their way out."

Kazuron shrugged. "No way to know in advance. We'll just have to handle it cautiously."

'We'? Especially given how they were treating her in this conversation, absolutely the fuck not. She might have needed Kazuron's connections to get this far, but this was *her* problem. Jesra didn't need to drag him any further into this with her—and she certainly wasn't going to let him run her.

She wasn't a student. She was a sword left too-long mounted on the wall and by all the gods, she was drawing herself.

She'd been waiting on a sign? Well, here it was. A sign she'd waited too damn long to admit what she'd known for years.

No one would ever accept her. There was no future for her in Eremor as a firestarter, and they didn't deserve her anyway.

But she'd make them choke on it.

The gentry would rue the day they thought they could use her and toss her aside. She wasn't waiting anymore.

Some bridges needed to be burned, and she was the firestarter to do it.

She *would* go back, she decided. She would face Bleic head-on.

But first, Jesra had slavers to hunt.

"The slavers are here for me," she told Kazuron. "I'll handle it on my own."

He frowned at her. "How are you going to stop them from—"

"They can't do anything if I burn them first," Jesra drawled lazily, cutting him off. "How far is Rimepeak from here?"

"Too far for the amount of fuel we have," Kazuron bit out.

That 'we' again. She turned to deliberately to Hansul. "Can I buy more?"

The tavernkeeper's gaze darted between her and Kazuron.

Kazuron said, "*We* are not going straight there."

All right then. Jesra faced the legendary swordsman square on. "You said it yourself, there's no way to know more without going there. I need information, and I will get it."

"Bullshit," he snapped. "You're going to confront them as soon as you see them. You won't help anyone if you get yourself killed."

Jesra's temper rose. "Do you think I'm incompetent?"

"No," Kazuron growled, "I think you need a plan."

Easy, Jesra. "I am not one of your students to manage."

"Clearly not, or you wouldn't be arguing with me."

Jesra snapped, "So that's what you want from people, just more minions?"

Hansul sucked in a breath.

She'd gone too far. She should apologize.

But as long as Kazuron didn't seem sorry for treating her like a child, she couldn't make herself do it.

They glared at each other.

Finally, Kazuron unhinged his clenched jaw far enough to say, "Let's finish this outside."

Well, that she could agree with. They didn't need an audience for this.

The snowglider was out there anyway.

"Thank you for the bread and your help," Jesra said to Hansul.

"My pleasure," the tavernkeeper said neutrally.

Not 'of course' or 'you're welcome' or 'any time'. Kazuron had a better friend than he realized.

She nodded in acknowledgment that she understood exactly where his loyalties laid and didn't hold it against him. Then she headed for the door, not waiting to see if Kazuron followed her.

But he did. As silently as he moved, she could still *feel* the dangerous presence of him at her back. The fact that it thrilled her only pissed her off more.

They were silent all the way back to the snowglider, and only then did Kazuron accelerate, overtaking her in a quick burst of speed and getting to the driver's side of the snowglider first.

She scowled up at him, fire dancing on her fingertips.

Kazuron raised his eyebrows and nodded back toward the tavern.

Hansul stood in the doorway, watching.

Jesra scowled harder, trudged around to the other side, and got in with bad grace.

Kazuron didn't test her patience, firing the snowglider up and heading back off across the vast expanse of white without delay.

"You know it's too soon to go," he said without preamble. No mention of what she'd said to him, which oddly made her feel worse about it. "You haven't recovered from being drained yet, and the slavers clearly haven't given up on you. They'll be prepared."

"And every second I wait is another they can prepare more. Every second is another they can use to enslave other people, because *I didn't act*."

"That's what you're on about?"

"Of course it is," Jesra snapped. "I was afraid to burn bridges out of my own selfishness—"

"And if I hadn't been so unwilling to get involved, people would have known they could come to me and it never would have gotten this far."

Jesra wasn't sure if that was true, that they didn't know.

But it didn't change the fact that he still didn't want to get involved with people, did it? And he shouldn't have to. He'd chosen his life already, and she wasn't going to take that from him.

But it was time to choose hers.

Kazuron put a hand on her shoulder. "You don't have to get yourself killed out of misplaced guilt."

She shrugged him off. "You're not responsible for me."

"Is that what you think this is about?"

"It's why you brought me out here," Jesra said, exasperated. "Your whole obligation thing, with the boots—"

Kazuron waved an arm. "I brought you here so you could have choices!"

"And I'm making them!" Jesra yelled back. "You want me out of your life, well I will damn well go—"

The snowglider slammed to a halt.

Before Jesra could ask what the hell was going on, Kazuron had hauled her into his arms and kissed her.

It was so sudden, Jesra was surprised into losing her train of thought.

And so welcome, she didn't try very hard to hold onto it.

A few minutes later, Kazuron pulled back to growl, "I do *not* want you out of my life. I do not think of you as a dependent. And I will absolutely not let you do this alone."

Her heart pounding, Jesra tried to gather her anger, her thoughts, about whatever the fuck had just happened. Was happening.

"I could, though," she said.

"You could," Kazuron agreed. "But you deserve someone guarding your back."

Oh. *Oh.*

Not as a ward. As an *equal*.

Jesra swallowed hard over the lump in her throat. She wanted that so badly it *hurt*.

"You left that life on purpose," she forced out. "It doesn't have to be you."

"I left that life," Kazuron said, "to make my own choices about who I fight for. I want it to be me."

"*Why?*"

He visibly struggled with it for a minute, and Jesra let him, waiting silently as the energy—from their fight, from their kiss, from her *need*—thrummed through her with the strange sense that whatever he said next was going to be direly important.

"I'm a cranky man who lives alone in the woods," Kazuron said gruffly. "You deserve to see the world and have all the adventures you want. But."

He swallowed; let out a huge gust of breath:

"But I still want you to stay."

Another stab right in the heart, and this time she didn't cover it at all.

No one, in her entire life, had ever wanted her to stay.

And—this was also the first time *she* had ever wanted to stay, too.

Jesra took a deep breath, as her heart hammered so wildly she could practically hear it. "Why do you think I want to be used any more than you do? I can skip that part of my future."

Kazuron looked he couldn't quite dare to hope she meant what he thought she did, and her heart squeezed as he ventured cautiously, "You wanted to do something that mattered with your skills."

"Tomorrow I am going to go kill an entire band of slavers and free an occupied town," Jesra said. "How does that not matter?"

After that—

For the first time, Jesra began to feel the shape of an idea she could live with. No—that she *wanted* to live.

Kazuron blinked, and his whole face lightened with relief. "Tomorrow?"

He might not be so relieved once he realized what she had in mind.

If he was serious about wanting her to stay, she'd have time to ease him into it. She *had* just crashed into his quiet life like a firestorm.

But he was volunteering—no, *insisting* on keeping himself in the heat.

"I'll give recovery one more day," Jesra told him. "But I'm more recovered than you think."

"Oh?" Kazuron asked, a heartbreaking smile that made her toes curl spreading across his face. Maybe he'd be an easier sell than she thought. "Prove it."

That last sentence dimmed her growing happiness. "Why should I? I'm not one of your students."

Kazuron smirked, an expression that activated parts of her that had already seen so much excitement in the last day but apparently were still eager for more, as he started the snowglider moving again and said, "Definitely not. But didn't you want to drive?"

And then he *let go of the wheel*.

Jesra yelped and grabbed the controls with her magic, firing the inner workings of the snowglider without physically touching the wheel.

When she glared at Kazuron an instant later, he was grinning at her.

Jesra swore at him, but she was laughing.

He'd known she could. This wasn't a test.

A second later she realized she was wrong, and it was a test after all.

Because he'd dropped to his knees on the floor of the glider and started removing her boots.

Oh gods, was he serious?

Jesra's heart sped up.

So did the need inside her.

"Since you can drive, and you know where you're going," Kazuron said, "let me give you a reason to want to come home with me."

She already wanted that.

But she absolutely did not stop him as he lifted her without even straining and pulled down her pants.

Kazuron ran his hands up and down her legs, feeling the unusual warmth of her skin. He raised his eyebrows up at her and Jesra found herself uncharacteristically flushing, but of course she was warm for *him*.

Then Kazuron began kissing his way up the inside of her thigh, amused eyes watching her the whole time, to see if she would lose control.

Jesra's breathing quickened, but she was fine. She was not going to crash a snowglider her first time driving because of one unbelievably dangerous man.

And she was still fine as Kazuron stroked her through her underwear, though her skin heated further and Jesra *knew* he felt it. He had to, because he kept stroking her in teasing circles on her leg, like the first time.

But it was *different* this time, because of the heat in his gaze.

And that Kazuron did it at the same time he palmed her sex.

Jesra could feel her wetness increasing and squirmed against his hand, but she was still fine. It would take more than that to break her concentration.

Then there was a sudden rip as he literally *tore off* her new underwear, who even *did* that, and she gasped—in surprise, at the quick blast of chilliness of the wind between her legs, and how incredibly turned on she was.

Her gaze snagged on his, and he locked his eyes onto hers.

Jesra didn't dare to breathe.

Then, very deliberately, never breaking eye contact, Kazuron licked her clit. A quick flick of the tongue.

Jesra arched out of her seat, but his strong hands gripped her hips and hauled her back down to his mouth.

She forgot her own name as her eyes rolled back in her head from the sensation as he feasted. There was no other word for it.

Jesra writhed, and Kazuron spread her legs wider, holding her open for him. She couldn't get away from his tongue as it scorched the deepest part of her and she didn't want to—it was so good, and she was so hot, but she was still not letting go of the fire directing the snowglider—

And then, lightly, *so* gently, he bit her throbbing clit.

Orgasm ripped through her and she soared.

Literally, because while she did *not* let go of the controls, she erupted so much power into them that the snowglider shot forward fast enough that it left the ground.

Kazuron didn't miss a beat, and his mouth never stopped.

Until the waves of pleasure finally crested and began to taper, and he dared lift his head to grin at her.

The sight of that expression on him, the Deathwind—*Kazuron*—between her legs, almost had her coming again right then.

Except the snowglider started falling.

Quick as anything, Kazuron wrapped his arms around her and leapt out of the snowglider, carrying her with him and rolling them through the snow as farther away the snowglider thumped messily to the ground.

Kazuron started to climb off her to check her for injuries, but Jesra grabbed his head and hauled him back for a scorching kiss that left both of them breathless.

"Life with a recluse," she teased. "So boring. Can't think of anything to recommend it."

His wicked smile lit her up, but then like a goddamn gentleman he *did* get off of her, throwing himself to one side with a put-upon sigh and wrapping an arm around her to help her sit up cradled against him.

That wasn't *so* bad, and Jesra's heart melted a little bit. Another time she would stay just like this for hours, and she planned to.

But not now.

They'd landed on a hill, their fall padded by several feet of snow, and Kazuron looked over the snowglider critically. "All in one piece, it looks like. I paid enough for that thing it ought to be sturdy."

"Doesn't matter how sturdy it is if it's on its side."

Kazuron shrugged. "I can flip that back over."

What the fuck.

Oh sure, just casually pick up a whole damn snowglider.

Of course he could. The man was unbelievably strong. And right now, Jesra had another use for that.

"Not yet," she told him.

Kazuron looked at her in query.

"If you can move it that easily," she said, "I don't think it's sturdy enough."

The slow, teasing grin that spread across his face made her heart turn over. "Oh? For what?"

Jesra reached over and gripped his already-hard cock through his pants, satisfaction thrilling through her as his breath hitched.

"For you to take me," she said, "as hard as you can."

Kazuron's eyes darkened as he tightened his hold on her, his cock somehow hardening further under her palm as his teasing grin dropped away.

Desire pulsed in her core, and Jesra turned around in his hold, onto her knees. She arched her back and looked at him over her shoulder with a grin. "If your pants aren't off in the next five seconds, I'm burning them off."

Kazuron swore, shoving them down as she laughed.

But when he caught her around the waist again and pressed against her, she broke off with a gasp.

"This?" Kazuron asked in a low voice, nudging her entrance. Teasing her. "Is this what you want?"

Jesra sunk lower into the snow on her elbows as she spread herself wide for him.

But she still looked back and met his eyes as she said clearly, undeniably, "This is what I want. Now, Kazuron."

"Always such a rush with you," he mused.

His hands stroked up from her waist, finding her breasts and circling them with his palms through the fabric and still teasing her entrance, making her rub back against him, desperate for more.

Just when Jesra thought she might actually have to set something on fire to relieve her frustration, Kazuron covered her whole body with his, flush against her and said roughly in her ear, "But I'll give it to you."

With a flex of his hips, he pushed into her, just the tip of him, and Jesra scrambled at the snow for purchase.

Kazuron squeezed her breasts, holding her in place as she panted.

He thrust again, farther in. And again, and again, working into her.

Jesra moaned at the feeling of all of him filling her up so slowly, inexorably, turned on even more as she heard him groan behind her.

And then finally, when he was all the way in, he paused. Jesra breathed in the feeling of him so deep inside her, of feeling so *full*, and held her breath, holding onto this moment and holding still, so still, waiting for him to—

Kazuron pinched her nipples.

Jesra arched with a gasp, and he pulled almost all the way out, but before she could miss him he *slammed* back into her and she screamed.

He stopped. "Okay?" he panted.

Jesra could have laughed that he thought he needed to ask, that he couldn't tell. But it was so him, trying so hard to take care of her, that instead she found her eyes filling with happy tears as all her feelings swelled and crested within her.

"Yes," she managed. "More, as hard as you can. I can take all of you, Kazuron."

He still didn't move, and she wondered for a moment if she'd gone too far.

But as pulled back he said, "Prove it," and thrust all the way into her in one powerful movement, making her see stars.

"My pleasure," Jesra managed to get out, and it was the last coherent thing she said as he began pounding into her in earnest.

With the force of every thrust they sank deeper into the snow, but it melted around them with all the heat Jesra was radiating.

She was in literal and metaphorical freefall, the feeling of being wholly and completely with another person who could take her, as she could take him, and she surged into another orgasm.

Kazuron kept going, letting her get ahead of him and chasing her through it like he knew he could always catch up to her, match her.

When he finally came, bellowing as he thrust powerfully into her and setting her off again, Jesra wasn't sure whether it was his force or hers that left them in a crater surrounded by walls of snow, the hill they'd been on top of now hollowed out.

Kazuron pulled her into his lap, cradling her as they both caught their breath and Jesra burrowed into his broad chest.

Kazuron murmured into her ear, "You can melt the snow around the glider to get it back on its wheels without me straining myself to lift it, can't you?"

Now he was getting it. Jesra smiled against his chest. "Yep."

Laughing more freely than she'd ever heard, Kazuron bent down and kissed her.

Now, for the first time in her life, Jesra felt like she could stay somewhere forever.

But first she had to go.

Chapter 5

They made it back to his cottage, cleaned up, ate, and slept. The next morning, Kazuron woke up holding Jesra in his arms on purpose, both of them having chosen to be there when they'd gone to sleep, and staying.

He held that knowledge close, waking her with light butterfly kisses so at odds with how forcefully he wanted to hold her and never let go.

But Jesra's sweet smile as she woke and saw him undid him.

They made love slowly, like they both wanted to prove to each other they would have all the time in the world, that this never had to end.

But end it did, with a kiss that Kazuron hoped felt more like a promise and less like desperation.

She would choose him or she wouldn't, but first she had to be free to choose anything.

And for that, they had business to take care of.

It turned out it took a *lot* more fuel to get to Rimepeak, and Jesra understood better why Kazuron hadn't been too sad when he'd stopped needing to do supply runs all the way there.

It also went some way toward explaining why the slavers had chosen that town—in addition to what Kazuron finally told her he'd noticed about the mercenaries, and what he suspected it meant, which also went some way toward explaining why he—and Hansul, who knew better what pressures non-humans found themselves under in the Five Protectates—hadn't been asking the same questions she had.

If Rivnian gentry were blackmailing the Fanged Host into slaverunning, that answered some questions—what they were doing out here, and maybe why they had some asshole humans among them—but begged many others.

Not just what the blackmail was. Like what men Kazuron otherwise thought of as decent people were doing to keep Rimepeak quiet.

Questions they could speculate on, but couldn't answer until they arrived.

And then Jesra would have to be prepared to make some decisions very quickly.

But they did, finally, after hours of travel, arrive, passing a tall tower that Kazuron told her was normally lit with a huge flame on top to serve as a beacon for travelers, or those fleeing Rivnia.

It was, unsurprisingly, not welcoming anyone to Rimepeak now.

And it would have made them easy to find.

Far easier than they could have found Kazuron in the Frozen Wilds.

Jesra had prepared herself to turn on the charm, briefed Kazuron with a cover story and everything, and all of it was for nothing, because as soon as they walked into town, absolutely no one would meet her eyes.

Anyone she approached turned their eyes to the ground and scurried away without a word.

All the while, Kazuron tried to make himself smaller.

He looked away, as if he thought if he wasn't looking at them they wouldn't be afraid of him. He stood farther back, still close enough to support her, but giving the illusion—to someone who'd never seen him use a sword—that he was out of range.

After the third time, Jesra had had enough. When a man tried to run from her, she darted in front of him and blocked his path, trapping him in between her and Kazuron.

The man's eyes widened.

"Why won't anyone talk to me?" she demanded.

The villager's eyes darted around.

"I imagine," Kazuron said, as the villager froze, "they've been instructed not to speak to us."

A door slammed. "Leave him alone," a woman barked.

Jesra turned to look, and the man took the opportunity to bolt.

"Nomin," Kazuron called casually. A middle-aged, stout woman with brown skin, pointed ears, and a no-nonsense apron glared back. "So nice to see you again. My friend has a few questions—"

"Your friend can take her questions and haul out of my town."

Okay. Time to take things up a notch.

"Is it your town?" Jesra asked. "Because if so, I *really* have some questions for you."

Nomin whistled, and townspeople emerged from their shops and homes, slowly forming a wall that began to close in on them.

If the town had been this organized before the slavers, Jesra doubted they could have taken Rimepeak. Nomin had learned, too late.

She murmured to Kazuron, "So much for them being too afraid of you to stand up to you."

"I don't like that they're defending the slavers," he said.

"I wonder if they are," Jesra said thoughtfully, casting her senses around.

Kazuron tried to raise his hands in a gesture of appeasement, but Jesra stopped him. "No, that's not the way we're playing this now. Let them see both of us as monsters."

Only when he paused and met her eyes did Jesra realize how firmly she'd said that, how she hadn't hesitated to take control, to choose a strategy.

He had more battle experience than her in one specific way, but she'd been fighting a different kind of battle for a long time.

She could play an audience.

And after how she'd handled Driftfall, Kazuron knew it.

He swiftly shifted to a quick hand on his sword, and the approaching townspeople paused as one.

Jesra smiled lazily and lit a flame on the end of her pointer finger.

They stepped back.

"Don't you dare threaten us," Nomin growled. "I told you to get out of here."

And that, if she really was working with the slavers, was a damn strange position for her to take.

"The slavers are looking for me specifically," Jesra said, "and they won't be happy you kept me from them."

The townspeople shifted but didn't clear out. "I don't know what you're talking about," Nomin snapped, but her face had tightened further.

Jesra focused on a nearby building, and once she was sure there were no heat signatures in it from anything living, she set the whole thing on fire at once.

Or it looked that way, anyway—in reality, the fire was only around the building, not touching it.

But they wouldn't know that.

Townspeople exclaimed and backed away; several held one man back who was yelling, so it must have been his. Jesra ignored it and looked at Nomin. "I can light up one building for every minute of my time you waste. There were no people in that one, but what about the next?"

Jesra pointed her flaming finger around the group slowly, as if deciding where to fire.

"Please," Nomin said. "We don't need this."

Jesra approached her slowly, pleased the tough old bird didn't back away, and very deliberately said, "I can light *anywhere* on fire without a thought." Her eyes bored into the town leader's, willing her to understand as she asked quietly, "*Where should I start?*"

Nomin's eyes widened. Thank the gods.

Then the woman swallowed and whispered, "The travelers' light beacon. It's over a well. But there are mercenaries guarding the top and bottom—"

Jesra didn't hesitate. She lit the two people on watch at the top of the tower on fire, and although they jumped out, she burned them so hot they were ash before they hit the ground. The guards at the base followed, and Jesra transferred the fire from the nearby building to the tower, surrounding it like a wall.

"They're dead, and anything on them burned with them," Jesra told Nomin. "That fire won't touch the tower, but it will keep anyone away from the well."

Nomin stared from the towering flames to Jesra, her face gone slack. Some of the townspeople had collapsed in what she thought was relief. "It was poison," she choked. "They would have poisoned our water—"

"I understand, but now *you* need to get away, because they're definitely not going to waste any more time setting up an ambush for us now."

Nomin swallowed. "Thank you. I'm sorry. Good luck to you."

Jesra smiled tightly at her. "I won't need it."

The woman regarded her. "Maybe you won't, at that." A pause and then she whispered, "The mercenaries saved the children, and we helped hide them. That's why the Rivnians are here now—to make sure no one they paid for gets 'lost'."

A threat, and a chance bundled in one. No wonder Rimepeak had been quiet.

As long as the mercenaries kept coming through this town, none of the other towns full of people who'd fled to the Frozen Wilds would be threatened, and some of the people taken as slaves would have a chance.

Rimepeak had been trying to save as many as they could.

That resembled the woman and people Hansul had thought they were.

Jesra told the woman quietly, "They lost me. And they're going to lose everyone else, too."

Nomin swallowed; nodded sharply.

And then got all the townspeople moving faster than Jesra would have expected anyone could herd cats, but these people had not been through an ordinary experience.

"I don't understand, actually," Jesra noted to Kazuron. "Why's the well special? There's snow everywhere."

"There's *ice* everywhere, and they're far from sources of wood," Kazuron said. "Used to be more when the town started, but a blight got to it. That well has a damn expensive firestarting spell to keep it from freezing."

"Expensive?" Jesra echoed, appalled. "That's *robbery*. I can do a spell like that in minutes."

"And they'd love you for it, and it ought to be more accessible than what folks out here are charged, but how long did you train to be able to do that spell in minutes? And how long would it take you to travel out here to do it, during which time you wouldn't be able to take on other work? Don't undervalue yourself either."

Jesra pursed her lips. "I see I have some things to learn about freelancing."

"Future problems, Jesra," Kazuron murmured, nodding toward the inside of the deserted town. "They'll be coming from that way."

"What makes you sure?"

"In my line of work, you learn to read tells," he said.

And the townspeople had been effectively blocking them from view in that direction, she realized.

They'd been trying to save her, like they couldn't save themselves. Like they couldn't save enough of the people who'd been taken.

But she didn't need saving.

"Let's move," Kazuron said. "We need cover, or they'll ambush us."

He definitely had more experience than her with this kind of battle.

But still, Jesra looked around.

She had good visibility. She'd had time to take stock of her surroundings.

And she strongly objected, on principle, to hiding from these fuckers.

So she told Kazuron, "Let them. I'm not running."

Rather than arguing with her, Kazuron swore under his breath. "Everything's always so dramatic with you."

Jesra relaxed and grinned at him, and the sharp understanding was like a punch right in his gut.

She hadn't been able to allow herself to be dramatic before, but with him, she could.

Kazuron vowed right then that he would always have her back so Jesra could be as much of herself as she wanted.

And he was coming to understand his firestarter always wanted to go bigger.

"You love it," Jesra told him. "When's the last time you had a challenge that would let you show off like this?"

Kazuron snorted, even as her words pricked him somewhere he hadn't felt in too damn long.

With her, it was safe for him to always go bigger, too.

At his cottage, he knew the ground like the back of his hand and had all kinds of backup measures if anyone ever tried to send a substantial force after him.

Here, though...

Here it was just him, and his sword.

And his firestarter.

Kazuron was much too professional to grin, but he did crack his neck with a kind of glee singing in his blood as mercenaries surrounded them on all sides.

Maybe he wasn't ready to be fully retired after all.

But then, from the direction he'd expected the ambush, more people came to the front.

Hostages. *Children.* Dirty, with dull eyes.

That was also why the townspeople hadn't taken more risks.

"Humans are the ones holding the kids," Jesra said to him quietly, barely moving her lips. "Mercenaries are the others. Anyone you recognize?"

"As a matter of fact," Kazuron said, not bothering to be quiet when one man in particular stepped forward, "I do."

Two days ago, this was one of the respectable mercenary bands he'd have referred Jesra to.

She'd been right before, that it wasn't the time not to appear to be monsters.

But it was true now, too. And this, Kazuron knew well how to do.

"Semyr," Kazuron growled to the commander of the Fanged Host. "What in the hells happened to you?"

Semyr's sword didn't waver, and he met Kazuron's eyes without flinching. "Rivnia took our families hostage. They have our children, Kazuron."

Damn it all to hell, he *knew* they'd had to be desperate.

Didn't change that they'd still participated in enslaving people, but this changed the perspective a hell of a lot.

"You should have come to me," he said.

Semyr shook his head sharply. "Any outside interference, our families die. Couldn't risk it."

"I could have—"

"I didn't know where you were," Semyr snapped. "I did my best. I *know* it isn't enough— believe me I know—but not all of us are legendary swordsmen, Kazuron."

That took him out where a sword in his gut wouldn't.

Kazuron knew he wasn't responsible for the world.

But he could have done something about this, when no one else could.

"And yet," a cruel voice he recognized crooned, "here you are, spilling secrets, silik. You know what that means."

Of course. Of course it would be him.

One of the reasons Kazuron had wanted out so badly in the first place.

And now this operation, running through the territory he'd fled to—

Naldis smiled at him, and Kazuron knew this wasn't an accident.

But Semyr's expression caught his eye. Resigned—relieved?

"I do," he said, holding Kazuron's gaze.

Fuck.

Semyr expected every single one of them to die.

It was why, when Naldis would have demanded a group of them corner Kazuron in his home, Semyr hadn't stinted. He'd known Kazuron would be ready; he'd also believed his men were already as good as dead.

Every one of the Fanged Host—but also every man Naldis had brought with him, before they could carry word of Semyr's "betrayal" back to Rivnia.

Semyr was counting on Kazuron to make that happen.

Sacrificing all of them, for the sake of their families. To stop this slaving operation from continuing.

If Kazuron had been a firestarter, he'd have fucking exploded right there.

But first, there was Naldis.

"I see," Naldis murmured. "I always knew siliks would prove unreliable. Unfeeling lizards who don't care about bonds of family, good only for one thing."

He meant death.

Semyr stiffened, but didn't go for his sword, which meant there was something else Kazuron didn't know about yet.

"Naldis," Kazuron snarled. The man's eyes narrowed as Kazuron deliberately didn't use any honorific for him. "How unsurprising to find you behind this."

Jesra tensed slightly at the name Naldis—good. He hadn't been sure how much she knew about international politics, but apparently it was enough to recognize Naldis' reputation as agent of the shittiest lord in Rivnia. Probably she knew of him as a cautionary tale.

She'd be more on guard, but with Naldis, that didn't matter. He was one of the reasons Kazuron had gotten out to begin with, so Naldis couldn't weaponize him.

But that hadn't stopped Naldis. He'd just drafted other tools.

That stopped today.

"Deathwind," Naldis responded with an easy grin. "I wonder how creaky you are, rusting away out here in the ass back of nowhere."

"I'd be happy to show you."

"Oh, I'm sure, but, well, it would be such a shame if one of my men here got nervous." A slaver struck a match and held it over the kids, who shrunk back, shimmering in their grime.

Jesra sucked in a breath. "They're covered in firestarting fluid."

God *damn* it, that's what the shine was. The same thing he filled his snowglider with.

That was why Semyr wasn't moving against them, even though he'd already signed his own death warrant.

And that was why they thought Jesra wouldn't just set them all on fire.

She didn't hesitate to snuff out that slaver's match, but on cue three others lit theirs.

And more closed in with torches.

It would only take one of them barely a flicker, and the children would go up in flames. Doused as they were in firestarting fluid, if Jesra used fire at all they'd catch, no matter how controlled she was.

"I see you understand the situation," Naldis said, still smiling. "Now, Kazuron, lovely as it always is to visit with you, our clients' quarrel is with the firestarter. With these odds, we could take your head as well, and don't think I wouldn't be just tickled pink to do so, but we're willing to let you walk back to your icy little prison."

Kazuron rolled his eyes. "No, you aren't."

Naldis laughed. "I had wondered if you'd gone stupid. No, of course I'm not."

Semyr tensed, the sudden realization that he might have brought Kazuron a problem too big for even him to handle, inflicting his own death sentence on the man he was counting on to save him.

But Naldis continued blithely, "I can solve your boredom problem. You return with me to Rivnia—"

"No," Kazuron said.

"No? Not even to save the poor defenseless lizards?" he taunted.

"No," he repeated.

There was no bargain that would keep them safe. Kazuron hoped Semyr understood that by now and didn't do something desperate.

Naldis' eyes narrowed again, and Kazuron knew then beyond a shadow of a doubt that gaining control of the Deathwind was why he was really out here.

Semyr thought he'd brought Naldis down on Kazuron, but it was Kazuron who'd brought Naldis down on Semyr.

After a moment, Naldis smiled again and lifted a hand.

But rather than speaking, one of the Rivnian soldiers fired a bolt at Kazuron without warning.

The Deathwind drew his sword and sliced through the arrow in the air in a single movement.

Finally.

"At last, we get to the goddamn point," he growled.

Naldis shrugged. "You only speak one language. If that's what it takes to make my point that you don't have a say in this, we'll do it your way." He raised his eyebrows and called, "If the Deathwind raises a hand to any Rivnian, light up the children." Naldis wore a small smile. "You don't want that on your conscience, do you? Such a tragedy you would cause."

No: It wasn't Kazuron who had brought Naldis down on them.

He wasn't responsible for evil.

But he was responsible for standing up in the face of it.

Naldis wasn't his problem. Not really.

But Kazuron was about to make himself the Five Protectates' problem.

Semyr lifted his sword, too, but it was aimed at Kazuron.

The human slaver grinned wider.

"Let me guess," Kazuron said. "You'll also set them on fire if any of the Fanged Host doesn't fight me."

Naldis shook his head. "It would be so regrettable, but when dealing with savages, we must have some insurance to keep ourselves safe. If you would all be reasonable, none of this would be necessary."

Right. No more talking.

Kazuron had protected himself when he left all those years ago, but he hadn't protected anyone else, not really.

He'd thought removing himself as a weapon would be enough to save lives, because he wouldn't be killing them.

But that wasn't good enough.

He *was* the Deathwind.

It was past time to make that matter. To take the epithet he'd grown to consider a curse, and make it his own.

Whatever Jesra thought in truth, Kazuron *was* a monster.

And he was tired of being sorry for the wrong things.

Kazuron never looked away from Naldis as he said, "Jesra, if you wouldn't mind sharing the fun, I missed my morning exercise. I think the Fanged Host will do for a warm-up."

He didn't know what she could do about the hostages, but with that much fire near them, she *had* to be the one to sort it out.

He'd only seen glimpses of what she could do, but he trusted her to handle it.

Jesra didn't even look at him, her eyes focused intently on the Rivnians. "Of course," she drawled, "I wouldn't want you to be *bored*."

Despite it all, Kazuron grinned at that, rolling his shoulders.

Naldis was too late.

Jesra had already solved his boredom problem.

And now, he was working again in truth.

The fight began in earnest, then, and Kazuron demonstrated why he still merited that damn epithet.

Not just because he was death, but because he was the wind.

He and his sword tore through the Fanged Host, his movement never ceasing. No matter how fast the mercenaries closed in around him and Jesra, no matter that they showered him with arrows, his sword was too fast.

Mercenaries fell in a circle around them. He kicked them away as they collapsed to keep his maneuvering room, but still they began to pile.

There were a *lot* of mercenaries.

Well. There *had* been.

But the Fanged Host wasn't stupid, and when he cut them down without killing them—a much more challenging task for him than simply meting out death, but he'd already been legendary before he'd retreated and trained *every damn day*—they stayed down.

He'd left to make his own choices about who to swing his sword for.

What he'd done with that time was teach students, not kill them.

He'd trained every day to be sharper, to be more precise, to be faster.

He could still deliver death, and oh, he would.

But only on his terms.

Because part of choosing was who to stand in front of.

Who to use his sword *for*.

That was where the real challenge came in.

But Kazuron's blood sang as he flew in a ceaseless whirl around Jesra, the center of the storm, never letting it touch her, as her concentration never wavered.

When the tide around him stemmed, he saw that even with the firestarting fluid, Jesra's control was *so* good that she could manage to set the slavers on fire without the fire touching the kids. It took all of her concentration, but she could do it.

Because she trusted him enough to have her back so she *could* devote all of herself to a challenge equal to her.

And Kazuron was not going to fail her in this.

He was a whirlwind but, for once, not of death.

And that only lasted as long as Naldis didn't realize what the fuck he was up to.

As long as he kept the focus on him, made himself appear to be the greatest danger, Jesra could work her magic.

Naldis was here for her, in theory, but he was obsessed with Kazuron, and now, for once, Kazuron used that to his advantage.

Eventually, though, the only ones left to face him were Rivnian, which meant the distraction game had just gotten much harder.

But finally, Naldis was no longer smiling.

He'd have at least realized that if Kazuron could tear through the Fanged Host's ranks so easily, and Jesra could nullify the threat to keep him in check, that not only was Kazuron even better than he'd been the last time Naldis had seen him fight, but that Naldis had a big fucking problem on his hands.

His insurance had been insufficient, and he'd underestimated the monster he'd sought to control.

But Naldis still drew his sword and closed with Kazuron, which meant he had at least one more trick up his sleeve.

Kazuron was a fighter, not a duplicitous shitbag, so while *not* killing in a fight was hard for him, facing Naldis directly was actually a bigger problem.

Naldis' swordsmanship was a cut above the average mercenary, so Kazuron wouldn't have let down his guard anyway. But since the man wouldn't know an honorable duel if it stabbed him in the face, this probably meant he'd dipped his sword in silik poison, so he couldn't let it cut him—and he'd have to clean his own sword before he cut anyone again that he wanted to live, too.

Fortunately, that did not in any way apply to Naldis.

"I see you still remember how to get your hands dirty," Naldis sneered.

Good; he hadn't noticed the Fanged Host weren't dead then.

"And yours are still covered in shit."

Strike; block. Just a testing blow.

"You always thought you were too good for us," Naldis said, "but here you are, caught up in the same game."

Kazuron wasn't going to point out that he wasn't playing the same game; he wanted Naldis' attention focused right on him.

"I *am* too good for you."

Not because he hadn't done his share of shit. But because he *cared* about it. And he'd ultimately chosen a different path, and not only because there was only one way Naldis' ended.

And today, he was choosing a different one still:

Not holding the monster he'd made of himself back.

Naldis laughed as he closed in again—he was quick, but as big as Kazuron was, Naldis still wasn't faster. "You'll get yours, Kazuron. You think the gentry will suffer you to live alone in peace out here once they know you're working again?"

Oh, he knew. His peace was at an end.

Jesra had thought her enemies too big for him, but *his* enemies were the real problem. He knew what getting involved again meant.

But Kazuron had left his former life behind to make choices he could live with. Come what may, there was only one choice he wanted to make now.

His sword in the wind, his blood singing, and his firestarter behind him.

Anything was worth it for this.

He would take his legacy and make something new with it.

If he could thread this damn needle, anyway.

Killing everyone quickly was a hell of a lot easier.

Kazuron knocked Naldis' next strike aside firmly, easily, and the next one.

That meant this was almost over.

Not because he was about to win, but because once he'd pushed Naldis just far enough—

"Let them come," Kazuron said.

And only then, when Naldis was sure Kazuron wasn't going to budge, when he thought he'd correctly assessed Kazuron's current speed, did Naldis get to the goddamn point.

His sword arm didn't falter, but with his other hand he squeezed a jet of poison at Kazuron.

Not from the sword after all—he must have realized what Kazuron would suspect.

But Naldis still didn't understand how fast Kazuron was.

He couldn't set individual drops on fire like Jesra, but he could use his sword to redirect the flow.

Unfortunately, it jetted toward one of the fallen mercenaries, who instinctively rolled out of the way.

Naldis' face went slack with shock.

And then it filled with fury.

Fuck.

Now the real fight began.

Naldis targeted Kazuron with the poison, the weapon it was harder for him to deal with, while aiming his sword at the targets Kazuron had left unable to defend themselves or scramble away.

Which meant Kazuron had to be in two places at once—defending all of them. If he slipped, not only did Naldis win, the Fanged Host would die, too, before they had a chance to correct what they'd unwillingly helped wreak.

Casualties of how blind he'd been to what he needed to do with himself. One more notch of horror in the Deathwind's legend.

Kazuron would die, too, of course. He could have accepted that, except that it would leave Jesra alone.

Jesra, who'd crashed into his empty world and lit the fire back inside him.

Unconscionable.

That thought, or the combination of them, unleashed him.

Like he was breaking through chains he'd unknowingly placed on himself, Kazuron moved faster than he had in his life.

The Deathwind in truth.

But with one very specific target, and he closed in.

Naldis was smart enough to recognize what was coming for him, but not why it hadn't arrived yet. He thought he still had room to maneuver.

He spat, "The gentry of all Five Protectates will decide you're too much trouble to live and will join forces, and even your reputation won't keep you safe from their combined resources—"

"Oh," Jesra said sweetly, "they won't have those for long."

There.

That was his death warrant signed.

Jesra had handled the rest of the Rivnians' threat, and that meant there was no more need to keep using Naldis as a shield.

In one flash of movement, Kazuron ran the mercenary captain through, and then shoved him, wide-eyed off his sword.

Before he'd finished dying, Semyr, using his sword as a cane to lift him up, slashed Naldis' throat with his claws.

Naldis began foaming at the mouth, and black spread from his throat through his body.

He was done, and Kazuron didn't need to watch anymore.

Coated in blood, he turned to Jesra, who used both her hands to tug him down for a fierce, consuming kiss.

Kazuron wrapped his free arm around her, grinning against her lips when he heard the crackle of arrows burning around them, followed closely by more screams.

This was the only place he wanted to be.

When they finally separated, there were no Rivnians left to flee.

A lot of their heads lay on the ground though, sitting in the ashes of their former bodies. Kazuron looked at Jesra inquiringly.

"I thought I'd bring the gentry of Eremor a token of my appreciation for introducing us," she said. "Maybe let the villagers and mercenaries stab them a few times first."

Terrifying as their sword and fire show might have been, the villagers hadn't wasted any time rushing back out. They wiped the kids down with blankets, applied healing salves, cut off ropes. It hadn't taken them long to free the other captives, either, and while those people weren't from here, the villagers spared no effort on them.

Solidarity, or apology; either way, these people would all, finally, be able to move forward.

And then they turned to help the mercenaries, too.

Semyr tried to refuse, and Nomin snapped, "All I have to do is sit on you to keep you where you are. You have children to save, and you'll be ready."

Semyr looked at him for help refusing help from the woman whose town he'd brought trouble to, and Kazuron drawled, "If you think I'm going to gainsay Nomin in this mood, you're not as smart as I thought you were."

As always, it was the wrong thing to say. Semyr's expression shuttered.

Nomin glared at him.

Goddamn it.

Like with Hansul, Kazuron didn't have smooth words, but he said gruffly, "I trust you to figure out what needs to be done for your people, and for the slaves you couldn't save."

Now Semyr looked like Kazuron had stabbed him, and Kazuron continued with a growl, "And now that you know where I live, if you need me, I trust that you will damn well *fetch* me."

He likely would need Kazuron's help. But Semyr and the Fanged Host needed to be the one who led this, for their sake.

Semyr hadn't meant to survive, and he probably wouldn't believe that he deserved to. But with at least a temporary goal in front of him, where his continued life performed meaningful penance, the Fangs might make it long enough to work through some of that.

From the tremor in Semyr's steady sword hand, Kazuron knew he was beginning to appreciate the enormity of what was ahead of him.

So he turned his scowl on Nomin and added, "You, too. Hansul realized something was wrong and would have come here unprepared soon enough."

Nomin stiffened, but nodded sharply.

Jesra put in more diplomatically, "If you can restock us on fuel, we can start doing a run for more healing supplies. I'm sure Hansul will have those ready by now, and I don't know much about bandaging, I'm afraid."

Now it was Nomin's turn to look almost choked up, but before the feeling could take her she turned and started barking orders.

Jesra backed them a thoughtful distance away, giving them space, and Kazuron tightened his arm around her.

It felt like events were already running away from him, but there was a big question he needed her to answer that had the potential to change everything.

"So. Healing supplies, sending a message. And what then?"

Jesra turned in his arm, looking out over what they'd wrought.

Kazuron knew he would have to go talk to people again, make sure everyone did feel safe, that he hadn't missed something crucial that they needed, and Jesra would help with that.

But in this moment her answer felt like the most important thing in the world.

Lightly, Jesra responded, "You mean assuming I don't bring an army to your door?"

That wasn't an answer, but it wasn't a rejection either. Yet.

"I would never assume that," Kazuron told her, "and I'm sure you can help me plant as many bombs as it takes."

Jesra's eyes widened and then she laughed, leaning her head against his bloody shoulder. "Let's do that, then."

Kazuron's heart fluttered as he looked down at her. "Yeah?"

She smiled back at him softly. "Yeah."

Epilogue

Approaching the guards at the city gates of Eremor, Jesra flung back the hood of her cloak.

The guards startled. "Jesra! We heard—" The man broke off.

"Oh? I'm curious, what is the gossip?"

They exchanged looks. "That you decided you were too good for Eremor, turned traitor, and left to sell yourself to the highest bidder."

"Ah, of course. Not that I was drugged in my bed and kidnapped by slavers. Curious, of course, how that managed to happen with a city watch such as yourselves on duty." Jesra grinned as they sputtered, a sunny, alarming grin. "Don't worry. I'm back to clear all that up."

The guards exchanged glances once more. "We don't have permission to allow traitors in the gates. Even if it's a misunderstanding," one said apologetically.

"Oh, of course, of course. Well, in that case, I need to get on with it as I have other business today, so you should stand back. Metal can get quite hot."

One guard frowned at her. "You're not thinking of forcing your way in? These gates are proof against fire, Jesra. You know that."

This time, her grin wasn't sunny at all.

Jesra extended a hand and the metal gates glowed a molten orange.

And then began to melt.

"They're not proof against fire as hot as I can make," she said softly.

The guards reached for their weapons only to find them also melting, and quickly divested themselves before they themselves caught fire.

Jesra didn't wait, sailing through the molten metal around her.

This simplified things, really.

If they'd declared her traitor, they'd have confiscated all her things, so there was no point going to her room.

Straight to the court chamber it was.

The guards eventually got the alarm sounded, but by then Jesra was already inside, striding through the halls.

She didn't fling any more fire. More guards closed on her, and any that got close found their weapons melting, their belt buckles burning.

A few firestarters attempted to approach her and rapidly backed away at the heat she was letting off, smart enough to tell when they were outmatched.

So no one managed to touch her before she arrived at the court chamber, already in session with a flurry of chatter.

Jesra didn't stop at the doors.

"Hello, old friends!" she called. "I understand there's been a bit of confusion about my sudden leave-taking. Lord Bleic, it was *so* thoughtful of you to make me aware of the local slaver problem. I've taken the liberty of resolving it."

The court burst into scandalized murmurs.

Bleic went white.

But quickly enough he'd pasted on a look of victimized outrage.

"Careful," another lord called to her. "That's quite an accusation to make of a nobleman, firestarter. You don't want to alienate this court's good opinion—"

"Where was the court inquiry when I was kidnapped in my own room? Where was the outcry against the accusation I'd turned traitor?"

She wasn't shaking, but it was through sheer will.

She'd never spoken against them like this.

She'd lived among these people for years, done everything they asked, done it not just well, but *amazingly*.

And this was all it got her.

Let anyone else like her understand before it got them, too.

"If this is the extent of the court's honor," Jesra said, "it is worthless."

The hall erupted.

But when Bleic stood and raised a hand, they quieted.

They knew who held real power here.

They knew not to rock the boat.

Jesra did too, of course.

But that knowing was wrong.

And she was going to rip the bandage off in an attempt to force herself to unlearn that all at once.

"The firestarter has challenged not just the court of Eremor's honor, but mine specifically," Bleic said smoothly, descending from his seat. "I will answer it for us once and for all."

Hook, line, and sinker.

She'd offered him another opportunity to get rid of her on a silver platter, where none would gainsay him killing her, and he'd be able to show definitively that he was the best among them.

They moved to the center of the court hall, spectators all around. Another lord marked the start of the duel.

Bleic took advantage of his moment in the spotlight. He spiraled flame all around him, a maelstrom of fire, playing to the audience.

Flame lashed toward Jesra, but she was a firestarter, too, and prepared, so his fire did nothing more than bounce off her ineffectually.

He had expected that, of course. He was building the audience up to appreciate his superior power.

But he'd already demonstrated enough for *her* show, so she didn't need to wait for the rest.

She wasn't playing his game anymore.

She was playing *hers*.

Jesra pointed a finger at Bleic.

And he lit up in a column of blue-white flame, his expression comically surprised, just for a moment.

Then he was ash.

The silence in the court this time was shocked.

And, for the first time, tinged with fear of her.

Maybe someday she'd be tired of that like Kazuron, but right now, as furious as she was with all of them, Jesra didn't hate it.

But she'd made her point. Bleic had stood for all of them, and as he was supposedly the best of their generation, she'd just demonstrated in an instant that she was far more powerful than they'd realized.

Into the stillness she said, "I gather Bleic's fabrication that I'd turned traitor means that my things were seized. You will reassemble and return them to me with all haste, or I will return to inquire why."

Finally one lady dared ask, "Where... will you be?"

Jesra smiled one more time, and the whole court froze.

"You can find me with the Deathwind," she said, and the court gaped.

Anyone who had been thinking of coming after her would be rapidly recalculating now, but Jesra still, smugly, put one final nail in the coffin.

"The Deathwind and I are open for business."

There was no resistance as she left court. She'd made her point.

And now, past the destroyed gates, utterly abandoned of a pretense of guards as pools of metal still smoked on the ground—

The Deathwind was waiting for her back in the bright snow, leaning against the snowglider.

"Was it as dramatic as you hoped for?" Kazuron drawled.

Jesra huffed. "Accused of dramatics by the man lounging here casually like he could lay siege to the city alone with just his giant ass sword."

"I'll take that as a yes." He smirked as she stuck her tongue out at him. "We're all fueled up. You can take us wherever you want to go."

And that might have just been the biggest difference between the world she left behind her and the one she was heading towards.

Jesra walked up and kissed him softly, smiling as he groaned.

Then she jumped in on the passenger side. "Home, then."

His smile was so bright Jesra felt her smoldering anger melting away.

Fuck Eremor. They weren't worth more of her energy.

Not when she had him.

Kazuron climbed in next to her. "Home it is, then."

Home.

She'd needed to come back here one last time—for closure, for vengeance, for staking her claim on the life she meant to lead. In a culture that cared about appearances first, publicly shaming them for involvement with slaving meant it would be much harder for Rivnian slavers to do business here, and that was the first stand she was taking.

But for the rest... there was one more tiny world-changing loose end she needed to tie up.

As the snowglider shot into the snowy expanse of freedom before them, Jesra took a breath and said, "I told them we were both open for business. I didn't specify that it was separately."

Kazuron glanced at her. "Good. Because it isn't."

Jesra blinked, momentarily derailed. "I thought I was going to have to work you up to that."

His lips curved. "Don't know why it took me so long to get my head out of my ass and realize. You need someone's reputation to get you started, and mine sure as hell is big enough. There are a few things we should work out between us—"

"I can think of a few, yes," Jesra murmured.

His smirk widened. "—*but* the principle is simple, as far as I'm concerned. You and me, doing whatever we want, together."

Jesra felt like her whole body was a smile.

She very carefully did not burst into happy flame—

But then on second thought, maybe just for a second.

Kazuron laughed out loud.

Unlike the people she'd lived most of her life among without killing any of them, Kazuron knew what she could do *and* wasn't scared of her.

It was going to take some getting used to.

"Well," Jesra said, "you *have* had a couple of less boring days. I'm sure your brain will get used to it eventually."

He snorted, but the look he directed at her was more serious. "There are some downsides to tying yourself to my reputation."

There it was.

"Oh, no, I'll have to take on problems big enough to trouble the Deathwind." Jesra rolled her eyes. "Please, that's a selling point. Any fights that come for you are fights that matter, and you can't say I'll be bored."

A pause, and then he asked, "And if I invite those fights?"

She knew what he meant.

If the Deathwind let it be known he was taking a stand in the Frozen Wilds, and that he was taking only select kinds of work, and that he was not willing to be wielded by anyone else but that they couldn't stop him from wielding himself...

Well.

They'd be busy.

Jesra returned his seriousness. "Then they're fights that need to be won, Kazuron. And if you think I'm going to let you fight them without me at your side, you haven't been paying attention."

She watched him closely, and then—

His shoulders *relaxed*. "I have been," he murmured. "But I didn't want to assume."

He wanted to fight *with* her. Not for her, and not sidelining her from the hard parts.

That made all the difference.

Struggling to recenter herself from the fight she'd braced for that hadn't materialized, Jesra shoved his shoulder. "Assume more, then. You're not getting rid of me that easily."

Probably not at all, if she was honest with herself, but this thing between them was new and Jesra didn't want to put too much pressure on it too soon.

Kazuron would probably tell her to assume more, too. But daring to believe he actually wanted her to stay at all, let alone forever, was a start. Maybe someday she wouldn't have to brace every time she tried to choose for herself.

In fairness, she had also had a couple of very not boring days.

Kazuron cleared his throat. "I haven't heard from Semyr yet, so we probably have time to do something before he needs us. If you don't want to wait for jobs to come in, there are a few people I could contact."

"Maybe later." She'd keep it in mind. But first she was going to take advantage of some space—and she *had* that space, now—to decide how to go about the future she wanted. *With* him. "You know Eremor may decide the two of us together are too much of a threat and try to wipe us out before we've even had a chance to get started."

Kazuron shrugged. "At least that won't be boring."

And then he tossed her a small package.

Jesra unwrapped it curiously.

"It's a cake," Kazuron said. "The frosting's in the middle, so it doesn't get mussed when wrapped."

Even before they'd decided anything, he'd been paying attention to what she wanted and arranged celebratory dessert for her.

For the start of her new future.

Their new future.

Her heart so full Jesra thought her face might crack from how widely she was smiling, the laughter burst out of her.

She reached over and held his hand as she took the first, perfect bite of her future.

Kazuron squeezed back, a soft smile playing on his lips.

She leaned in close to share that bite with him, too, and then kissed the sweet taste off his lips as they continued into their bright new future together.

Thank You

Thank you for reading! And special thanks to Lisette Marshall for giving me the nudge I needed to finish whipping this book into shape.

If you enjoyed reading this Firestarter and Swordsman book, I hope you'll tell someone about it or leave a review!

For FREE, newsletter-exclusive short stories, sign up for my newsletter at caseyblair.com! Subscribing will keep you in the loop on free fiction opportunities, sales, and new books—including what's next for Jesra and Kazuron.

You can also join my extremely low-key reader group on Discord where we share book recommendations, cat pictures, and sneak peeks of my works in progress.

Happy reading!
Casey

Take Back Magic

Enjoyed this book? Don't miss *Take Back Magic,* the first book in the completed, action-packed modern-day fantasy romance Diamond Universe series!

WHEN LEGENDS SPARK

Earth's magic was stolen. She's taking it back.

All Sierra Walker has ever wanted is magic, but the powerful mage who trained her as a child betrayed her, sending her back from a world full of magic to modern-day Seattle. So when he comes to her a decade later, Sierra glimpses an opportunity:

She steals his wand, and with it, she begins to steal back magic—for *everyone*.

In magical combat Sierra's a force to be reckoned with, but she's still on her own, her access to magic handicapped, with an entire world of mages now trying their best to kill her rather than share power. So when Nariel, a dangerous demon lord, offers his assistance, she can't say no. But she also knows better than to trust her life, and her magic, to anyone else ever again—no matter how he ignites a part of her she'd thought long lost.

But as they race around the world to bring magic back while fighting for their lives, Sierra realizes there may now be two things she can't bear to lose.

Diamond Universe: Sierra Walker is a fast-paced, action-packed urban romantasy series spanning the modern world and also other worlds full of magic, with a shadow-wielding demon boyfriend and a heroine who never quits no matter the odds and just goes harder as they fight to change the universe for everyone. Expect the heat level to escalate dramatically in each book.

The Sundered Realms

For another action-packed, romantic epic fantasy, check out the first book of the Sundered Realms series!

Liris has always been too dangerous to be allowed freedom. Now she's the universe's only hope.

Liris has been trapped training as an elite spy her whole life. But when her elders try to sacrifice her to further their own interests, she escapes through a secret portal—only to land right in the hands of Lord Vhannor, the most dangerous spellcaster in the universe.

Vhannor has dedicated his life to defending the universe from world-devouring demons, and Liris, with her unique knowledge of an ancient spell language, jeopardizes his mission. But when she uses it to help him close a demonic portal before it can destroy all life in that dimension, he's forced to acknowledge he needs her by his side.

As they race between dimensions to fight their mutual enemies, they discover a plot that will leave every remaining realm in the universe at the mercy of demons. But to stop it, Liris will have to rely on the man whose icy gaze sees right through her... and when even her own people betrayed her, how can she trust Vhannor to stand by her when she risks the whole universe?

The Sundered Realms is equal parts epic fantasy and romance in a world where being a huge nerd about language makes you incredibly epic at magic. This is an action-packed story about an interdimensional combat ambassador heroine and the most dangerous man in the universe devoting all his attention to making her unstoppable.

Tea Princess Chronicles

Looking for cozy fantasy? Don't miss *A Coup of Tea,* the first book in the completed, bestselling Tea Princess Chronicles series!

When the fourth princess of Istalam is due to dedicate herself to a path serving the crown, she makes a choice that shocks everyone, herself most of all: She leaves.

(Start Reading)

In hiding and exiled from power, Miyara finds her place running a tea shop in a struggling community that sits on the edge of a magical disaster zone. But there's more brewing under the surface of this city—hidden magic, and hidden machinations—that threaten all the people who've helped her make her own way.

Miyara may not be a princess anymore, but with a teapot in hand she'll risk her newfound freedom to discover a more meaningful kind of power.

A Coup of Tea **is the first book of the Tea Princess Chronicles, a cozy fantasy series full of magic tea, found family, baby dragons, and lifting people up even when the odds seem impossible.**

Also By

Diamond Universe: Sierra Walker
Take Back Magic
Take Back Demons
Take Back Worlds

Sundered Realms
The Sundered Realms

Tea Princess Chronicles
A Coup of Tea
Tea Set and Match
Royal Tea Service

Tales from a Magical Tea Shop:
Stories of the Tea Princess Chronicles

Stand-Alone
The Sorceress Transcendent
Consider the Dust

About the Author

Casey Blair is a bestselling author of hopeful fantasy novels about ambitious women who dare, including the Diamond Universe, Sundered Realms, and Tea Princess Chronicles series. Her own adventures have included teaching English in rural Japan, taking a train to Tibet, rappelling down waterfalls in Costa Rica, and practicing capoeira. She now lives in the Pacific Northwest and can be found dancing spontaneously, exploring forests around the world, or trapped under a cat.

For more information visit her website casey-blair.com or follow her on Instagram @CaseyLBlair.

Manufactured by Amazon.com.au
Sydney, New South Wales, Australia